Holiday

with the Players

REBECCA JENSHAK

Snowed in with the Player

Dedication

For my favorite twins.

Chapter One

STELLA AND I SING ALONG WITH THE HOLIDAY TUNES AS I make the last turn down the snowy street that leads to the cabin. Snow! It's quite the change of scenery from when we left Valley University, only three hours ago. The sun had been shining and we were sweating by the time we loaded up our Jeep for the holiday break. But here, it looks and feels like winter. I love it.

"I can't wait to sleep in tomorrow." My twin sister rolls the window down, letting in the blistery cold air. "We survived our first semester of college!"

"Yeah, we did." The smell of pine trees and brisk air fills the vehicle, and we breathe it in with matching smiles.

"This was a great idea. We can snowboard, ski, snowshoe, and—"

I cut in to add, "Read by the fireplace, bake cookies, watch movies."

Stella laughs. "We'll do all of it. It's going to be amazing." She rolls the window back up. "Have you heard from Felix?"

"No. I texted him before we left, but no response. Are we terrible for ditching him for the cabin this weekend?"

"Are you kidding? He probably has plans to throw a party at the house every night until Mom and Dad are back."

I nod my agreement, but I still feel a stab of guilt.

Our parents are in Cabo until Christmas Eve, taking a

much-deserved vacation. They've been saying they were going to take one for years, and they finally did it.

It's weird not rushing home to do all the usual holiday festivities, though. I look forward to it all year—making sugar cookies and decorating them, watching all our favorite holiday movies, and just lounging around and enjoying my family.

Stella and I decided that since Mom and Dad are gone, we'd spend the weekend at our family's cabin in Flagstaff, unwinding after the long semester before going home. She likes to ski. I like to sit by the fire and read. It's going to be so much fun. Different, but fun.

Our brother Felix goes to Valley U too, but he finished with classes a day earlier than us and headed home to Scottsdale to housesit while Mom and Dad are gone. And Stella is right. He's probably stocking the fridge right now and preparing to throw a party.

We're quiet as we pass the ski resort. The parking lot is packed, and people walk to and from the front with skis and snowboards, dressed in warm layers.

"Ah, it just got real." Stella bounces in her seat, sending her ponytail swinging around her shoulders. "Tomorrow we should sleep in and then go up to the ski resort and buy passes for the weekend before they sell out."

"I don't know if I'm going to be doing that much skiing. I should probably stick to ice skating and snowshoeing."

"I'll go on the bunny hill with you until you get the hang of it again." Her excitement is contagious.

"Deal."

As the cabin finally comes into view, a familiar orange vehicle catches my eye.

"Uhhh. Are you seeing what I'm seeing?" I ask as I pull the Jeep to a stop behind Felix's Corvette.

"What is he doing here?" Stella gapes at our brother, standing on the porch of our grandparents' vacation cabin and wearing a Santa hat but no shirt.

"Freezing to death, from the looks of it."

He isn't alone. A group of people fill the small front porch. A couple I recognize as his football teammates, but the others I've never seen before. Knowing Felix, he's already made friends with the neighbors in the short amount of time he's been here. My brother can and will talk with everyone he meets. And he knows how to throw a party, so people tend to flock to him.

I kill the engine, and the holiday music we'd been listening to on our drive up from Valley U. The mood has officially deflated.

Stella hops out first, and with a grin that's half annoyed and half pleasantly surprised, shouts, "What the hell, Felix?"

She slams the door behind her and marches toward the cabin. People stare at her as she approaches. I slink down in my seat.

Felix looks surprised, but still smiles, even as Stella continues to shriek at him. His response back is muffled. They hug, but I can tell Stella is still worked up by the way she waves her hands around as she speaks.

Felix walks back to the car with her. I roll down my window and the cold air bristles against my face.

"Holly!" My brother greets me. His eyes are glossy, and he smells like he's been drinking for the better part of the day. "I can't believe you two are here."

"Same. I thought you were taking care of the house for Mom and Dad while they're in Cabo?"

"I am."

I get out of the car, and he pulls me into a big hug, squeezing me and lifting my feet off the ground.

"Funny. It doesn't look like you're in Scottsdale."

He ruffles my hair, which he knows I hate. "I've got it under control. Don't worry."

"Well, that just makes me more worried." I scan his bare torso. "You're missing a shirt."

"Spilled beer on it." Laughing, he looks from me to Stella and back again. "Why didn't you two tell me you were coming?"

"We texted you this morning after we were done with classes," Stella says.

"I was already here. We came up last night." He pats his front and back jeans pockets. "I have no idea where I left my phone."

"Typical," I tease.

He pulls me in for another hug. "This is rad. We can all hang out. How long are you staying?"

"Just the weekend. There is a good chance of snow. We thought we'd ski and hang out for a few days before going home." An excited smile tips up the corners of Stella's lips.

"And we thought the party would be at Mom and Dad's, since you're supposed to be housesitting," I chime in. "We can't all stay here. There isn't enough room."

"Sure, there is." My brother waves off my concern.

It's a rustic, two-bedroom cabin that's been in our family for three generations. Our great-grandparents bought the land when there was nothing else around. They built a summer getaway house to escape the brutal temperatures in June and July. The temperatures in northern Arizona are way cooler than just a few hours south, and this is where they'd come on weekends or time off from work.

That was before someone decided to build a ski resort half a mile away. It made the property worth a lot more, but it also meant that a dozen more cabins popped up all around. Most are rentals or vacation homes, but there are a few people that live here year-round.

We came here a lot as kids during the summer. And as we've gotten older, Felix, Stella, and I like to come up here in the winter with friends to ski or just hang out. During the winter break, it's packed with high school and college students. But it's been a few years since we've all been here together.

"Where are we all going to sleep?"

"We'll figure it out." Felix throws an arm around each of our shoulders. "Come meet some people."

Laughing, I shrug out of his hold. "I'll be right there. I'm just gonna grab some of our stuff."

Stella goes with Felix, and I walk behind the Jeep to get our things. I know my sister well enough to know she won't want to change our plans for the weekend, even if it means sharing the small cabin with our brother and his friends.

She will spend most of her time at the resort anyway, so it's not that big of an inconvenience, but my plans of enjoying the quiet and reading by the fireplace seem far-fetched now.

Plus, Stella and I might be twins, but when the three of us hang out together, she and Felix usually team up against me. They're both a lot more extroverted than I am, and deciding what to do quickly becomes two against one. It's the only reason I've gone skydiving or been to a dance club. It's not all bad. Sometimes they pull me out of my comfort zone, and I'm thankful, but other times, I end up anxious and sweaty. The dance club falls into the latter column.

I leave the suitcase in the back of the Jeep to get later, but grab two of the paper bags filled with food for the weekend. Some of it needs to go in the fridge—assuming it isn't already full of beer.

I'm wrangling a third bag, so I can get it all in one trip, when a familiar deep voice cuts through my thoughts.

"Hold up. Let me get that."

Teddy invades my space before I've had time to prepare for him. And where Teddy is concerned, I need time to prepare. His hand brushes mine as he takes the last bag from me, sending goosebumps all the way to my toes. I breathe in the scent of his soap, mixed with the winter wonderland around us, and it's just about the most heavenly thing I've ever smelled.

"Thanks," I mumble as I take him in.

Theo Radford. Star running back of the Valley University

football team, my brother's best friend, impossibly nice guy, and my secret crush.

It's silly, really. He's ridiculously handsome and, of course, super popular, and I'm just me. One of Felix's little sisters. The shy one, the one people overlook.

He's big and burly like a teddy bear, which is why everyone calls him Teddy. He's one of the few people that never makes me feel like the "other" twin. I like that about him. I like a lot of things about him.

Including the way the long-sleeved shirt he's wearing strains against his biceps and back. He's six foot, two inches, and every part of him is broad and muscular.

"How are you, Holly?" Even though lots of people can tell Stella and me apart, I secretly love when it's Teddy who calls me by name without prompting.

"Good. You?" My cold cheeks flame with warmth.

"I'm good. Nice antlers." One side of his mouth quirks up and his dimples are on full display. I love his dimples.

When Teddy isn't smiling, he looks tough and really intimidating. I've been watching him play football with Felix for the past two years and that tough and intimidating look has coincided with a lot of touchdowns. He is no-nonsense, all-out, determined, and aggressive on the field, but when he smiles, Teddy looks like the nicest guy you could ever meet. And he really is.

My hand flies to the reindeer antler headband I'd forgotten I was wearing, and I smile timidly. "Thanks. Felix didn't say you were coming to the house for Christmas again this year."

Teddy's from Virginia, a long way to fly home for the holidays. Last year, he came to our house. It wasn't the start of my crush, but spending so much time around him definitely kicked it up a notch or twenty.

"I'm not. I didn't want to impose on your family again. Lucas invited me to his folks' house for the break." He nods his head to our luggage, bringing my attention to his dark blond hair. It's thick and a little unruly, but it suits him. "The suitcase too?"

"I can get that later," I say.

"I got it." He reaches in and grabs it then starts for the laundry basket.

"Not that one," I say too late. The big, white basket is filled with dirty clothes that Stella and I planned to wash once we got to Mom and Dad's. A pair of my holiday panties with little gingerbread men and women all over them are on top, and I think I might die as Teddy quickly looks away and his cheeks go ruddy.

I take another step from the Jeep and Teddy shuts the back.

"Thank you," I say again as we walk up toward the cabin.

"No problem." He stops on the bottom step of the porch stairs to let me go first. "I gather you weren't expecting us to be here."

"Felix is nothing if not spontaneous."

"Sorry." He cracks a sympathetic smile as I pass by him. A dozen or more people stand on the front porch, drinking and talking.

Inside, the place is a mess. Empty beer cans litter the kitchen counter, the top of the fridge holds a row of liquor bottles, and next to the sink, shot glasses are lined up beside pizza boxes.

Teddy drops the paper bag on the counter and then hoists the suitcase up like it weighs nothing. "Where am I putting this?"

"I'm not sure." I scan the living room. Pillows and blankets are spread out on both couches and there's a sleeping bag on the floor.

"You two can have my room." He tips his head and starts down the short hallway with the second bedroom, and I follow him.

"You don't have to do that," I say as he sets my suitcase down next to the bed. Felix will have called the master. It's on the opposite side and has a private, attached bath.

"It's fine." He grabs his duffel bag.

"Where are you going to sleep?" I cannot picture him in a sleeping bag on the floor.

"I'll mange on the couch." He winks and it sets off a thousand butterflies in my chest. "Do you want a beer or something?"

"No thanks. Not yet."

He nods and heads back out. I linger in the bedroom for a moment to get my bearings. This trip is off to a rocky start. Are we all really going to stay here?

My fingers find the gold name necklace Stella got me as an early Christmas present. She got one for herself too. She said they were so people would stop confusing us. Our friends from high school could tell us apart, but since getting to Valley, we've had to go through the whole people confusing us thing again. It gets a little awkward sometimes when people get it wrong, and I have to tell them I'm not Stella.

We're only one minute apart and identical twins with matching long, strawberry-blonde hair and brown eyes with flecks of green. Staring at her should be like looking in a mirror, but Stella has that something about her that would make her stand out, even if every person in the world looked the same. She's fearless and fun, confident. Stella has always been into sports and social clubs, while I like to hang with a small group of friends and cheer her on from the sideline.

If we were the Wakefield twins, she'd be Jessica for sure.

I take a deep breath and force myself to stop hiding. I can do this. Everything will be fine. Felix and his friends are fun, and I'll be sleeping under the same roof as Teddy. There are worse things.

Teddy is in the kitchen, pouring himself a drink, when I walk out to the main room. It's open-concept, with the kitchen on one side and the dining room on the other. The living area sits in between with a TV over the fireplace. Sliding glass doors lead out from the dining room to a deck that looks out to the mountains, but the front porch is where people tend to congregate.

The TV is on and *Jingle All the Way* plays on mute.

"I love this one," I say, stopping in front of the TV.

Teddy's long legs eat up the space between us, standing beside me in three big steps. His arm brushes mine and I expect him to pull away, but he doesn't.

"Me too."

Captions are on and we watch silently for a few minutes before he turns to me. "What's your favorite holiday movie?"

"That is an impossible question."

A silent laugh shakes his chest. "Top three?"

"*Elf*," I start. "*Christmas Vacation*, and *Home Alone*."

He nods along. "All great choices."

"But then there's *The Grinch*, *Bad Santa*, *Love Actually*, *A Christmas Story* . . . there are so many good ones."

"*Die Hard*," he adds and then tilts his head to study me. "You aren't one of those people who claim it isn't a Christmas movie, are you?"

"Definitely not. It's *so* a Christmas movie."

He leans into me. "I knew I liked you."

His shoulder rests against mine and that winter-wonderland scent envelops me as he stares down at me with gray eyes. My body warms from his touch and his words. I'm suddenly unable to come up with anything to say back to him and an awkward beat passes between us while neither of us moves.

This might be the longest conversation I've ever had with Teddy. And the first one we've ever had alone like this. Sure, we've had one-on-one conversations before, but there were always other people around, aiding as a nice distraction in case I said something embarrassing.

Noise outside catches my attention, breaking the nice moment between us and reminding me we aren't really alone.

Teddy takes a step away. "Ready?"

I let out a shaky breath and nod.

Felix and two more of his teammates, Lucas and Emmett, are standing next to the door outside with girls I don't recognize.

My brother introduces me to Tricia and Anna. The girls wave around their red Solo cups. A couple of guys join us, and Felix introduces them to me as Brian and Kevin. He doesn't specify which is which, so I just nod and smile.

"We went to high school together. They go to NAU," Felix says, and then hangs his arm around my shoulders. "And this is one of my sisters."

One of the guys steps forward and extends a hand. "Nice to meet you. What's your name?"

Felix's voice turns protective. "Hey, hey. Don't get any ideas. My sisters are too good for any of you. This is—"

"Wait, let me guess which one." Lucas stares at me closely, then his gaze darts over to where Stella is standing on the opposite side of the porch. "You're Stella."

"Yep." Emmett nods his agreement. "Definitely Stella."

"It's Holly, you idiots," Teddy says.

"Really?" Lucas's gaze narrows.

I nod.

"How do you always get it wrong?" Felix asks with a shake of his head.

"They're identical twins," Lucas whines. "They look *identical.*"

Felix just laughs, but Teddy stares right at me as he says, "No, they don't. It's easy to tell them apart. You're just not looking close enough."

I'm on cloud nine until he adds, "Her name is right there on her necklace."

Chapter Two

STELLA THROWS HER HEAD BACK AND LAUGHS AFTER I tell her about my interaction with Teddy. The party died out and everyone who isn't staying here went home, leaving me and Stella alone with Felix and his teammates.

She glances over to where Teddy and the guys are tossing a football in the front yard. "I think it's great he's here. You will have a chance to hang out with him more."

"Oh, yeah. Another chance for him to not notice me." I don't even try to hide the defeat that spills out with my words. I have had a crush on Teddy since the moment I met him.

Felix is fifteen months older than me and Stella. He went off to Valley U while we were still in high school. I'll never forget the first time Felix introduced Teddy to us. It was after a home game. We'd all come down to watch Felix play.

It wasn't anything Teddy said or did. It was in all the things he didn't say or do. He is quieter and sweeter than the rest of Felix's friends. He smiled with those dimples, looked me in the eye and repeated my name like he was committing it to memory. That was all it took. I was smitten.

And every interaction, everything I've learned about him since, just makes me fall harder.

"Oh please, he totally notices you. How else did he see that necklace?" She lifts her chin and drops her gaze to it.

"He notices me, of course he does, I'm his best friend's sister, but he doesn't *notice* me. There's a difference."

"He was checking you out."

"I don't think that's what he was doing." My face heats.

"He's a straight, very hot-blooded college guy. He checked you out. He probably just thinks you're not interested because your default mode around him is to hide or barely say two words back to him."

It's true. I tend to freeze up around him. Teddy makes me nervous. When he talks to me, or anyone really, he gives his undivided attention. And all that attentiveness from a guy that already makes my insides feel like goo is overwhelming.

And okay, it isn't fair to say he doesn't notice me; Teddy is always friendly, but he doesn't see me the way I see him. I know, because he treats Stella the same way, like he's looking out for us because it's his obligation as Felix's best friend.

"Felix and Teddy are staying until the twenty-third."

Three nights longer than Stella and I planned.

"You want to stay?"

"Don't you? Teddy is here!"

I shush her, but my face remains hot.

"He isn't listening," she says with a small laugh.

"What about all our plans? We were going to do holiday stuff, like bake cookies and watch *Home Alone*."

"I know." She turns, so her body is angled toward me, her eyes pleading with me. "But if we stay, we can do all that and ski and hang out with Felix. What are we going to do at home by ourselves that we can't do here?"

I hesitate. The answer is nothing, but I'm still torn.

"Please?"

"Okay," I relent.

She squeals and her smile gets bigger.

"But we're getting a tree for the cabin, and you have to go with me on the bunny hill."

"Whatever you want," she says and hugs me. "This is going to be so much fun!"

Her phone pings, and she pulls back quickly to look at the screen. A goofy grin lights up her face. The kind of grin that can only mean a text from one person.

"Is he done for the semester too?"

"Yeah. He finished yesterday and flew home today."

Stella met a guy last month at the airport. She's a diver and was traveling with the Valley U Swim and Dive Team. Serendipitously, she ended up sitting next to Beau at the gate before her flight. He goes to college out of state, but is originally from the Phoenix area like us. Even so, I didn't really think anything would come of their happenstance meeting, but they've been talking all day, every day ever since.

"When do I get to meet this guy?"

"I don't know," she says. "He's only home for two weeks, and he has plans with his family."

Stella gets lost in her phone, and I go back to watching the guys. Felix throws the football to Emmett and calls, "I'm out. My nipples could cut glass."

He jogs up the front porch steps and heads inside. I follow after him.

"Beer?" he asks.

"No, but will you grab me a soda?"

He does and then cracks open his beer and starts toward the master bedroom.

"Wait." I walk with him, entering the messy room. It's decorated exactly as you'd expect from grandparents. Elementary school pictures of Felix, Stella, and me in all the awkward phases are framed on the dresser, and it has a smell that's a mixture of Icy Hot and floral potpourri.

"Stella and I are going to stay."

"Awesome."

"You're really not pissed we're crashing your entire week of partying?"

His blue eyes crinkle at the corners as he smiles. "Nah, but I hope you're prepared to sleep on the living room floor. At least until Sunday. Emmett is leaving then. After that, you are welcome to the lumpy couch."

He sets his beer on the dresser and pulls out clean clothes from his bag on the floor.

"Not necessary. Teddy already gave up his room." I smile smugly as I sit on the edge of his unmade bed.

"That Teddy." He shakes his head as his voice takes on a taunting edge. "I'm going to have to talk to him about being so nice to my annoying sisters."

"Teddy is nice to everyone."

"True," he says and then flicks on the bathroom light.

"What's the plan for tonight anyway?"

"Lots of drinking, then who knows. Wherever the night takes us."

Felix takes his beer and disappears into the bathroom. A second later, the shower turns on. I get up to leave, but pause in the doorway and say, "We should get a tree."

"A tree?" he calls over the running water.

"Yeah. You know, those things you decorate at Christmastime."

"Uh, yeah, maybe. I'm not sure how much room we have for that."

He's right. The cabin is not spacious, but our parents already said the only tree we're doing at home this year is the small artificial one mom puts up in the kitchen and decorates with Santa ornaments. She usually puts up at least five artificial trees throughout the house—ranging in size and color and theme, but my favorite is always the real one that goes up in the living room. I love going to pick it out, the way it smells and the way it looks all lit up at night. Stella and I planned to get one this weekend and surprise everyone, but then we decided to come here instead. All the good ones will be picked over before we get back.

"We'll make room," I tell him.

I only get a grunt in acceptance, but it's good enough for me. One small, Christmassy win.

Chapter Three

WE HANG OUT AT THE CABIN FRIDAY NIGHT, AND everyone goes to sleep pretty early. The next morning when I wake up, the guys are getting ready to go to the resort to ski, Stella too.

Felix smirks as he scans my sweatshirt. It reads, *Don't stop Believin'* with a picture of Santa Claus. "Did you get that for an ugly holiday sweater party or something?"

"What?" I gasp. "No. This sweater isn't ugly."

He chuckles. "Are you coming with us today?"

"And miss an opportunity to hang here by myself and read?" I shake my head. "No chance."

"You could come and sit in the lodge and read. Better view, better food, and we can hang out while I warm up between runs." Felix shrugs.

"Yeah!" Stella exclaims. "Come with us."

I glance around the messy living room. It isn't the cozy environment I had hoped for and the lodge at the resort is beautiful. Plus, they do have better snacks. "Okay. Let me grab a couple of books."

"A couple?" Teddy asks.

"She's a speed reader," Stella says proudly, like it's my superpower. Being a twin is funny like that. We both admire the things the other does better, even if it's something silly like reading faster.

We pile into two vehicles to head to the resort. As everyone else goes to rent gear and buy passes, I head to the lodge. It is my absolute favorite part of the resort. The restaurant sits off on one side, the bar on the other, and in between is a giant fireplace with lots of cozy chairs. I find one near the windows, overlooking the ice-skating rink. There's also an outdoor-seating area with a snack bar for those who want to grab something to eat, without taking off their wet gear.

Light snow is falling outside, and the sky is gray. I order a muffin and a coffee and take a seat with my book. I'm in the middle of a flirty romance and the hero is working hard to win over the heroine.

It only takes two paragraphs to suck me back into the story and I'm lost to the rest of the world. I don't look up again until I'm finished. I hug the book to my chest. It's the perfect way to spend the day, watching the snow, sitting near the fireplace, and finishing a great read.

I stand up and stretch and then pull out my second book. This one is a thriller set in a cozy mountain town in the middle of a blizzard. Curling up in the chair again, I just finish the first page when Stella flops down in front of me, bringing a blast of cold air with her.

"I missed this place." Her face is red, but her smile is huge.

"Me too."

She eyes the book in my hand. "Already on your second book?"

"Yeah," I say as Felix and Teddy join us. Teddy peels off his coat and gloves, and then rubs his hands in front of him.

"I need to dry off," he says, taking a seat.

"You only get wet if you fall." Felix grins. "I'm gonna get a drink. Want anything?"

"Nah." Teddy shakes his head.

"I'll come with you." Stella hops up. "I need something hot. I'm frozen to the bone. I should have packed some warmer clothes."

When it's just the two of us, Teddy stretches his long legs out in front of him and then takes the beanie off his head and runs his fingers through the thick strands.

"How was it?" I ask.

"Brutal. I let your brother talk me into going down a black diamond on my first day." He chuckles softly. "I think I rolled down most of it."

"You've never skied before?"

"Never. And from my performance out there this morning, I'm thinking I oughta stick to sports that don't require me to wear tiny sleds on my feet."

"There's also cross-country skiing, snowboarding—Stella loves that, or snowshoeing."

"Snowshoeing. Isn't that just like walking in the snow?" His gray eyes crinkle at the corners as he smiles.

"But with special shoes," I insist, then laugh. "They rent shoes and poles here for it. We should try it while you're here."

He stares at me a beat, without speaking, and I realize I've just suggested the two of us hang out. "I meant you should ask Felix to do it with you. Fair warning, he'll get bored ten minutes into the walk."

"Thanks for the heads up." His gaze drops to my book and then back up. "What about you?"

"What about me?" I squirm a little under his scrutiny.

"Which is your favorite winter activity? After reading, of course."

"I like snowshoeing. It's the only winter sport I don't feel like a complete klutz."

"You're not klutzy."

"Compared to Stella and Felix, I am."

"I heard my name," Felix says, plopping down into a chair next to Teddy. "Are you telling her how I kicked your ass on the slopes?"

"You got me," Teddy says with a chuckle.

Stella, Emmett, and Lucas are behind Felix, and they gather around in a circle, drinking and warming up. The snow stopped

18

and the sun is shining. It's the type of winter weather that makes you feel like you should get out and do something, instead of sit inside (well, not me, but other people) and as soon as the guys finish their drinks, I can tell they're antsy to get back out there.

"You ready to fall down some more?" Felix nudges Teddy.

"I'm almost dry."

"Come on, Radford." Felix stands. "You can't give up yet."

Stella jumps up, ready to go too.

"Good luck," I say and wiggle my fingers at a reluctant looking Teddy.

"I'm gonna need it." He slowly gets to his feet and groans, looking around the room like maybe he's appreciating it in here like I do, then his gaze stops on me. "Staying in here looks a whole lot better."

Chapter Four

THE GUYS START DRINKING AS SOON AS WE GET BACK from the resort, and by the time eight o'clock rolls around, they're ready to kick it up a notch. The liquor bottles come down and more people fill the already-cramped living area.

I'm sitting with Teddy and one of his and Felix's teammates, Garrison, who lives nearby and drove up for the night, watching them play something on the Xbox. The rest of the guys have set up beer pong on the dining room table. The other couch is taken by a group of girls the guys met the first night—Tricia and Anna, and a couple more I haven't been introduced to yet, and in the kitchen are more people I don't know.

Stella is hiding in the bedroom talking to Beau, so I'm doing my best to blend in until she's done.

"Do you need another drink?" Teddy asks as he gets up from the couch. Tonight, he's wearing a white Valley U football hat and his dark blond hair curls around his ears.

The hard seltzer in my hand is nearly full, but I say, "Sure. Thanks."

Anna rushes to take his spot. Her hair is long and blonde, and she smells like cotton candy. "Is he your boyfriend?"

"Teddy?" I ask, watching his back move to the fridge.

She quickly nods her head up and down like a bobblehead.

"No," I say, and immediately regret it because her eyes gleam with excitement.

"I didn't think so, but I wanted to be sure. Thank you!" She hurries back to her friends and tells them the good news.

I feel a prick of irritation and unease because I really don't want to be stuck in the same house as my crush while he hooks up with another girl, but when Teddy comes back and hands me a cold can and falls into the seat next to me, I push away my annoyance and move an inch closer to him.

"Same game?" Teddy asks Garrison.

"I think I'm out. I need to move around." Slowly, he moves his booted foot from the coffee table and grimaces.

Teddy leans back on the couch. "What's the latest word from the doctor?"

Garrison was injured in a football game earlier in the season. It was a nasty hit, though they all look pretty brutal to me. I cringe every time Felix gets sacked, which thankfully isn't that often.

"He thinks I can rehab it without surgery, but I have to wear this fucking boot for another week. I'm losing my mind."

Teddy stays silent, but nods. "Sorry, man."

"That stupid fucker Ricci is going down next year. He should have been ejected for that dirty hit." He gets to his feet and grumbles, "I need a shot or twelve."

"Is he okay?" I ask when he's gone.

"Yeah. His foot will heal, but he's gonna be pissed for a while."

"What did he mean about it being a dirty hit? They all look awful to me."

"It came late, after the play. Garrison was already out of bounds when Ricci took him down. It's tough for refs to call." Teddy continues, "Things out there happen so fast. Guys have a hard time stopping but sometimes it's just dirty." Teddy releases a breath and holds out the controller to me.

"I've never played this game," I say, but take it and sit up to place both of my drinks on the table.

"We can play whatever you want." He navigates back to the menu to show me the options.

"Have you ever been injured playing football? Aside from the thumb dislocation last year."

"Good memory." The smile he aims at me makes me dizzy. "Not like Garrison. No broken bones or injuries that have kept me sidelined, but I've had plenty of bumps and bruises. What about you?"

"Me?" I shake my head. "I was never into any sports, except swimming, and one summer I played softball with Stella." I shudder at the memory.

"I bet you looked pretty cute in a baseball cap." He takes the hat off his head and places it on mine, then leans back to get a better look at me. "Yep. I knew it."

"We wore visors." Frenetic energy courses through me. Being near Teddy, especially when I'm talking to him, has this weird effect on me, where I want to lean into the moment while simultaneously wishing I was invisible.

His smile widens. I leave on the hat. It's too big, falling over my eyes, but I don't care.

I place a hand to my cheek. "It's kind of hot in here."

He tilts his head to the door. "Want to step outside for a minute?"

I think the heat coursing through me is more from him being so close than the temperature in the cabin, but I nod. We abandon our spots on the couch and head for the front door. Teddy holds it open for me and I blush harder as I walk in front of him.

It hasn't snowed any more, but the front porch is still partially covered. We stand at the railing, looking out toward the tree line to the right of the cabin.

Teddy groans and rolls his neck.

"You can take three-hundred-pound dudes pummeling into you, but you fall to the ground on your own and turn into a big ole' baby," I tease.

"Yeah, yeah." He hits the brim of his hat, still on my head, and fights a smile. "I tried to keep up with your brother. That was a mistake. My ass is black and blue."

I laugh softly. "Seriously?"

"Seriously." He turns, so his back is against the railing, and looks over at me. "It's so peaceful out here. Feels like we're inside a Christmas movie."

"Yeah, I guess it does a little." I tip my head up to look at the stars. The cold is seeping in through my thin sweater and I hug myself for added warmth. "But we'd be the least festive house in the movie."

A rough chuckle leaves his lips and hangs in a cloud of cool air.

"We're totally festive. Felix is even wearing his Santa hat again." He gives his head a shake. "I made fun of him for it, but the girls flock to him in that thing."

"I'll tell you a secret about my brother." I lean closer. "Girls flocking to him might be a nice side effect, but he's wearing that hat because he loves Christmas. It's a Walters' family tradition. Felix and Dad wear Santa hats the entire week leading up to Christmas. My mom buys them in bulk."

"That's right. I remember that from last year. Why aren't you festive tonight? Did you run out of holiday sweaters?"

I brush my hair away from my ear and show him the dangly holly flower earrings. "And I have reindeer, Santa, Christmas trees . . . you get the picture."

"You Walters are freaks."

"We love the holidays. I'm having fun being up here, don't get me wrong. I love the cabin and the snow, but it doesn't feel like Christmas without being home."

"What's your favorite part?"

Some time while we were talking, we both angled our bodies to face each other. Teddy reaches out and takes my hands in his giant palms, then rubs lightly.

His touch throws me off for a second, and I think my brain short circuits. "Picking out the tree and then decorating it with our old ornaments. But I love other things too. Like how Dad and Felix put up lights outside, and Mom wraps all our presents in special coordinating paper. It's different every year, but the result is a work of art. Stella and I always make a bunch of cookies and we watch the first two *Home Alone* movies together."

"They made more than two?"

"They shouldn't have, but yes."

"That all sounds amazing. I was honored to be a part of it last year."

"I know it's silly, but I really look forward to it."

"That isn't silly at all, it's beautiful."

I want to ask him what his family does every year, and if he misses going home for the holidays, but the way he's looking at me makes speaking impossible. His gaze darts to my lips, and when it moves back up, there's an intensity swirling in his stare that wasn't there a second ago.

"There you are!" Stella says, opening the front door and peering out.

I'm slow to look, still too caught up in the guy in front of me. When I do, my sister steps out and then pauses when she takes in the scene in front of her. Teddy lets our hands drop.

"Am I interrupting?"

"No, I got too warm in there. Teddy stepped out with me for some cold air and then we got to talking."

"Oh." Stella's smile says way more than that one word. "Well, that was nice of you, Theodore."

He chuckles. "I better go reclaim my spot on the Xbox."

His eyes briefly flick to me before he heads back inside.

"You and Teddy!" Stella screeches as soon as the door closes behind him.

"No."

She hits the brim of the hat, *his* hat. I feel sort of silly wearing it now, so I take it off. "We were just talking."

"If you say so." Stella shivers. "It's freezing out here. We really should have brought warmer clothes."

I follow her inside to the kitchen. Stella grabs a bag of chips from the pantry and then an entire jar of salsa. "I thought we could watch a movie in bed? I'm exhausted. Unless you want to stay up and hang out."

I look around the party in the living room. Teddy is flocked on either side by Anna and another girl.

"A movie sounds great."

We watch *Elf* and eat the entire bag of chips and most of the salsa.

"I invited Beau to visit over break."

"Here?"

"No." She shakes her head. "After Christmas, before we go back to Valley. You're going to love him."

"That's great, and Felix will be there in case he's a total creeper in person."

"Yeah. Felix can meet him too. But he isn't a creeper. I met him in person, remember?" She laughs and falls back onto the bed. "I hope Felix is cool."

"Why wouldn't he be? He knows you date and make out with boys." I gasp and cover my mouth with my hand.

The party has died down and only the faint sound of the guys talking drifts through the walls.

Stella's quiet, only giving me a small smile. She's already so nervous for us to meet him, which tells me exactly how much she really likes him. The three of us are close. It would be hard for any of us to date someone the others didn't like.

"I can't believe you met a guy at the airport. Only you. Guys basically fall into your lap." I shove her foot lightly.

She sits up and grins at me. "It could be you if you'd actually talk to Teddy like you did tonight."

"Shh!" I glance at the closed door.

"Oh, relax. He isn't eavesdropping." She yawns and plugs her phone into the charger, then lies back down. "But seriously, this week is the perfect opportunity to make something happen."

Her eyes flutter closed, and I get under the covers beside her.

"Want to go get a tree in the morning?"

"Maybe. First, I want to sleep for like eighteen hours." She curls up on her side facing me. "Night, Holly."

"Night, Stell."

I fall asleep thinking about Teddy. I know my sister is right. I should do something, since we're sharing the same space for a few days, but making moves on guys is not really an area in which I excel. Reading, school, shoes, Christmas trivia, knowing the lyrics to every pop song on the radio—those are topics I am much more versed in.

And with Teddy, there's a lot at stake. He's my brother's best friend. If he doesn't feel the same, it's not like I can hide from him forever.

Stella is still sleeping when I wake up the next morning, so I quietly change and then take my toothbrush and makeup case out to the bathroom.

Noise from the television that was left on all night makes it hard to tell if anyone else is awake. Once I'm ready, I tiptoe through the living room. Emmett is lying on the floor in only his boxers, and Lucas is facedown on one of the couches. Garrison and the other guys that drove down must have left last night. The spot where Teddy slept is empty and Felix's door is open and the sliver of his bed I can see is clear.

"Morning." Teddy's deep voice rumbles through my insides.

I jump and place a hand on my chest.

"Sorry," he says as I meet his gaze. He leans against the counter with a tall glass of milk. He's shirtless and even though I've seen him like this before, I have a hard time not letting my gaze linger on his broad shoulders and tapered waist or the light smattering of hair that trails down his stomach and disappears into his sweatpants.

"Morning," I finally return his greeting, "I didn't know anyone else was up."

I glance toward Felix's room again. The bed is definitely empty.

"He'll be right back. He walked the girls back."

"Oh." I knew they were still here when Stella and I crashed, but it didn't occur to me until now that they might have stayed over. And if Teddy is the only other one awake . . . I shake away the thought. I do not need to picture Teddy or my brother hooking up.

I grab a glass from the cabinet and fill it with water, looking anywhere but at the guy next to me. He's had girlfriends before, but somehow thinking of him hooking up with a random girl hurts more. That random could have been me.

Felix returns, when it's borderline uncomfortable, and I have never been so glad to see him.

"Hey," I say cheerily.

"Morning."

"Just barely." The microwave clock reads ten fifty-eight. "I checked and there is a tree lot about a mile away."

He doesn't look stoked about my idea, so I continue to plead my case, "If we don't get one soon, they'll be sold out."

Felix kicks off his shoes and pulls a sweatshirt over his head. "No can do. I'm going to jump in the shower and then I have to go to Scottsdale. Mom texted last night. Apparently, she has carpet cleaners coming today."

"Did you tell her you were here?"

"No. Just said I'd take care of it." He shrugs.

It makes me smile, thinking of Mom worried about the cleanliness of her floors while on the beach.

"Are you coming back?"

"Yeah, we'll be back later tonight." He raises his voice, "Yo, Em, Luc. We're leaving soon."

Stella comes out of the bedroom, her eyes still half-closed. "You're going home?"

"Just for the day." He grabs a Gatorade from the fridge.

"Can I come with you? I want to do a load of laundry and grab some warmer clothes. I forgot how cold it gets up here."

"Uhh . . ." Felix starts, "it'll be tight, but I guess we could squeeze you in."

"She can have my spot," Teddy offers. "I'll stay here."

I glance between Stella and Teddy. "Stell, you can't leave. We were going to watch *Home Alone* and *Home Alone 2* today." My cheeks heat. I know it sounds silly, childish even, but it's a tradition. We always dedicate one day in the week leading up to Christmas to watch those two movies together.

"We'll do it another day," she promises.

"I could come too, and we could watch it on the drive."

"No," she says too quickly, "you should stay here. We'll watch the movies tomorrow."

She smiles, eyes wide like she's trying to communicate something. Usually, I know what she's thinking, even without that look, but right now I have no clue.

"Okay. I guess I'll bake cookies today and we can decorate them tonight." That's another one of our traditions I look forward to every year. I like to bake. Stella hates to touch the oven, but she sits and talks with me while I do it. Occasionally, she even helps decorate them.

My sister steps closer and grabs my hand. "Holly, can you help me find the concealer?"

"It's in the makeup case."

She takes a step toward the bedroom, tugging me with her. "Show me. I couldn't find it."

"We're leaving in twenty," Felix calls after us.

She drops my hand and shuts the door behind us. I walk straight over to the makeup case and pick up the concealer.

"I don't need the concealer."

"Then why did you ask me to help you find it?"

"So you would stop going on and on about cookies and movies. You are going to be alone all day with Teddy."

My face floods with heat, and I glance to the door. "Shhh!"

"Holly, this is the perfect opportunity."

"Spending the day alone with Teddy is the perfect opportunity to what?" I throw my hands up in the air. "I still haven't mastered talking to him without feeling like I'm going to pass out."

"So don't talk. Tear off all his clothes and kiss the man."

"Oh my god, Stell. Shhh." My face is on fire.

She laughs as I continue to freak out. "Your face is so red right now. Teddy is hot and nice and just . . . good, ya know? He's one of the good ones. Lots of girls want to tear off his clothes. I don't know why you're embarrassed that you're among them."

"Because he doesn't see me that way."

"I don't believe that for a second. Though he probably won't make the first move because of Felix. You're going to have to do it."

"Yeah, well, that's never going to happen."

Chapter Five

LUCAS STANDS FROM THE COUCH. "TRY NOT TO MISS ME too much, Hol-Stell-whichever one you are."

"Holly," Teddy and Stella say at the same time.

"Geez, dude. You've known them as long as Teddy." Felix shakes his head.

"Sorry." Lucas shrugs one shoulder. "But you told me not to look at them twice when we met, so . . ."

"He gave us all that talk," Emmett says, then looks at Felix. "So don't go blaming us for not being able to tell them apart two years later."

"Fair enough." Felix laughs and tosses a chin jut and smile at Teddy. "You're good staying?"

"I'm not squeezing into the back seat with those two," he says and points at Lucas and Emmett. Then he gives my brother an easy smile. "I'll be fine, man. I'm gonna ice my tailbone. Drive safe."

The door closes behind them and silence falls over the cabin. I'm alone with Theo Radford.

An entire day, just the two of us, in this cabin? Sure, that sounds like a dream come true, but that assumes a lot of things. Including my ability to form sentences.

"I'm going to shower." Teddy jabs a thumb toward the bathroom.

I'm rolling out cookie dough, proudly wearing one of my grandmother's old aprons, and listening to Christmas music.

I've known Teddy too long to feel uncomfortable being in the same space, but there is definitely a different type of tension when he comes out to the living room in jeans, holding his T-shirt in one hand.

"Hey, can you help me? I need to put some of this balm on my tattoo."

"You got a tattoo?" He's one of the few on the team that didn't have one. Felix has so many I've lost count at this point.

"Yeah." He smiles and those dimples make my stomach flip. "Two days ago."

Teddy invades my space in the kitchen and turns to show me. Over his left shoulder blade is an intricately drawn woman with large wings. She stands in profile with a fierce look on her face, a sword at her hip.

"It's beautiful. Does it have some significance?"

"She's my guardian angel. Figured it wouldn't hurt for her to have my back on the field, ya know? Plus, she looked awesome." He hands me a tub of tattoo healing balm.

"Your guardian angel is seriously hot and pretty badass."

His upper body shakes with his laughter. "No doubt."

I dip my fingers into the balm and then run it over the tattoo. His skin is warm and my heart races as I gently dab it onto the skin. The tips of my fingers linger there, tracing the outline of the black ink.

"All done?" His voice is deeper than it was a minute ago and the sound goes straight to my lower stomach.

"Yeah." I drop my hand and set the tub of balm on the counter.

I move to the sink to wash my hands and then go back to rolling out the dough.

Teddy puts on his shirt and then takes a seat at one of the stools on the other side of the counter. "I was thinking, if you want, I could go with you to pick out a tree."

"You don't have to do that."

"I want to. Plus, I'm not doing anything else today."

"What about that girl Anna? You aren't seeing her again?"

His brows pinch together. "Anna?"

"She was asking about you last night." I stare down at the cookie dough. "I thought, maybe . . ." I can't think of a way to finish that sentence without embarrassing myself, so I don't. "It's okay. I need to finish the cookies anyway."

"Okay." He gets up and goes around behind me in the kitchen to the sink. He turns on the faucet, but I don't look back to see what he's doing.

I finish rolling the dough and then begin to cut out shapes with holiday cookie cutters Stella and I picked up on our way to the cabin—snowflakes, presents, Christmas trees, reindeer, gingerbread men and women, candy canes, bells, wreaths . . . we went a little overboard. Okay, fine, it was mostly me.

Teddy appears by my side, drying his hands on a towel. "How can I help?"

He drops the towel and scoops up a scrap piece of dough and tosses it in his mouth.

He has a boyish grin on his face as I smack at his hand. "No taste-testing until the end."

"Yes ma'am."

"You really want to help? Don't feel like you need to hang out with me just because everyone else left. I'm fine on my own."

"I really want to, Holly. And for the record, nothing happened with Anna. She stayed because Tricia did."

"Oh." It's all I can think to say. My heart is beating so loudly, I'm certain he can hear it. Glancing down, I ask, "Do you want to use the cookie cutters or the spatula?"

"Whatever I can screw up less."

I hand him the spatula. "Put the ones I cut out onto the pan. Leave an inch or so between them."

I cut out more designs and Teddy uses the spatula to lift the cookies onto the pan. He curses as a Santa-shaped one sticks. He tries to help it off with his finger but mangles it.

"Shit."

"It's okay." I step closer to help reshape poor Santa. One of his legs sticks out at a weird angle. Somehow, in trying to fix it, I make it worse and now there's a bulge between Santa's legs. Perfect. I just made the cookie anatomically correct.

"Oh well, that one can be our taste-test cookie at the end."

He nods and tries another, getting a similar result.

"Here." I hand him the bell cookie cutter and step around him.

He is meticulous in his work, and we get into a rhythm, only stopping when I need to roll out the dough again.

"You really do this every year?" he asks, swiping another scrap of dough to eat.

"Yeah. We make sugar cookies, sometimes other kinds too. I basically live on sugar during the holiday break."

He laughs. "Sounds nice."

"What about you? What kind of things does your family do for the holidays?"

"It's just my dad and brother and me. It's pretty low-key. Nothing like the Walters' family traditions. Definitely no cute, shaped cookies." He holds up a snowflake cookie cutter.

His mom died when he was young. Something I knew from Felix, but have never heard Teddy mention.

"You don't bake together during the holidays?"

"No. My dad makes two things—spaghetti and steak. The other nights of the week, we eat out or make sandwiches or something easy."

"And what about you?"

"I don't cook if I can help it."

"If I had to eat the same two meals every week, I think I would have learned."

"I like spaghetti and steak."

We both laugh.

"Those are ready to bake." I point to the pans.

I set a timer while he puts them in the oven.

"Ever made homemade frosting?"

He lifts a brow. "Didn't even know that was a thing."

"Do you like frosting?"

"Hell, yeah."

"Just making sure. It doesn't fall into your spaghetti or steak diet."

We move around the kitchen. I get out the ingredients, he gets the measuring cups, and together, we make enough buttercream frosting for twice the cookies we made.

I hold out the spoon for him to taste. He leans forward, his lips part and his tongue darts out, just before his mouth covers the end of the spoon.

He groans as he pulls away, eyes falling closed, making butterflies swarm in my lower belly.

"Good?"

He nods, eyes still closed. "So damn good."

I'm still staring at his mouth when he finally opens his eyes. I feel a ridiculous amount of pride at his praise.

The timer goes off and I quickly move to pull the cookies from the oven.

"Now we just have to wait for them to cool."

"And then we can decorate them?"

"If you want."

"I want," he says, and his gaze drops to my lips.

I step back, suddenly aware I'm covered in flour and frosting. "I'm a mess."

"Yeah, me too." He glances down at his T-shirt.

"I'm gonna clean up."

"Okay. Then, if you still want to, we can go get a tree."

I half expected him to duck out by this point. It's been a few hours since Felix and Stella left, which means they're home and the cleaners are working. My time alone with Teddy is running out.

"Okay." I blow out a breath. "Yeah, let's go get a tree."

At the tree lot, Teddy falls into step beside me and we slowly walk through the rows of firs and spruces. It's the perfect weather for tree shopping. The sky is overcast and there's a light snow falling. They have holiday music playing and lights strung up around the perimeter of the lot to add to the Christmas spirit.

"It's like being in a snow globe." I hold my arms out to my sides and turn in a circle.

"You really like Christmas, huh?"

"Doesn't everyone?"

"Everyone likes vacation and getting presents, but no, I don't think everyone really likes Christmas like you do."

"There's just something about it," I say, glancing over at him. The ends of his hair curl around the edge of the black beanie pulled down low to cover his ears. "It's magical. The lights, the smells, the cheer. Anything feels possible this time of year."

I feel a little silly immediately after the words are out of my mouth, but Teddy grins at me. "I like Christmas too. When I was little, my mom made a big deal out of it. I miss that."

"What kinds of things did she do?"

"She made gingersnaps. She only iced half of the cookie like they were dipped in icing. I don't know why, though. Maybe that's how they're supposed to be. And she collected snowmen." He smiles. "I forgot about that. They were all over the house."

"I love that."

We wander down the rows. It's busy today with families and

couples all picking out their perfect tree. I stop in front of a large Grand fir. It's beautiful. I lean in and breathe in the scent.

"That the one?" Teddy asks.

"No." I sigh and run my hand over a branch. "It's too big for the cabin and too pricey." I point to the three-hundred-dollar price tag. "Besides, Felix and Stella like the Douglas fir better, so we always get one of those. But this one smells better."

He steps closer, his arm brushing mine and he inhales. "Smells pretty good."

"Told you." I step away and head toward a section of smaller trees, many are shaped funny or not as full. A half-off sign hangs behind them.

"A Charlie Brown Christmas?" Teddy asks.

"These trees need love too." I wrap a hand around the top of the best of the ugly, unwanted Douglas fir trees. "What do you think?"

"I think if anyone can make that tree beautiful, it's you."

His compliment and the way he's looking at me turn my legs to rubber. Maybe Stella was right, and Teddy sees me as more than Felix's little sister. The thought makes me dizzy with hope. I take a step, wobble and fall toward him with the tree.

Teddy wraps one big arm around me, and with the other, he steadies the tree. I'm cradled against him. He's warm and sturdy, and the mixture of smells—the snow and the trees and *him*—renders me completely helpless.

"Are you okay?" I can feel the question rumble in his chest. I wonder if that means he can feel my heart racing.

Reluctantly, I step out of his hold. "Perfect."

Chapter Six

BY THE TIME WE MAKE IT BACK TO THE CABIN WITH THE tree, the snow is coming down and covering the ground in thick blankets. Teddy parks and I hop out and stare up at the sky.

I stick my tongue out and catch a large snowflake. When I glance back at Teddy, his hat is covered in white, and he's grinning at me. He leans down and scoops up a handful of snow with a wicked glint in his eye.

"Oh, no," I say as he packs the snow together. I get my own snowball ready, but he's quicker and a big, wet heap of snow pelts me in the arm.

We fire more snowballs at each other, running around the small yard. Mine all miss. He might be bad on skis, but he's quick on his feet. He comes at me and wraps an arm around my waist to keep me from throwing another at him.

"Truce." His voice rumbles next to my ear.

I swivel in his hold, our faces inches apart. His gray eyes twinkle with mischief and something else I can't quite place.

"Truce," I agree. He lets go of me and then I fire at close range. This one gets him.

He shakes his head and laughs. "Come on. We better get your tree inside."

Together, we carry it into the cabin. Teddy stomps back outside to shake off the snow. "It's really coming down out there."

"Yeah." I pull my phone from my pocket. "I thought Felix and the others would be back by now."

"Zero chance his car is making it on those roads until they clear them."

"Crap, you're probably right."

I FaceTime Stella. She answers, holding up our parent's cat, Whiskers. "Look how big he's getting."

"You're still in Scottsdale?"

"Yeah. The guys decided to play nine holes of golf while the carpet cleaners were here. They should be back any minute. How are things with—"

"You need to hurry. It's snowing. Like a lot. The roads are totally covered, and it does not look like it's stopping any time soon."

Her brows pull together in the middle, and she lowers Whiskers. "Hold on. Felix just got here."

I listen as she relays the info to my brother. A minute later, Teddy's phone rings. Stella and I are quiet while they talk.

Teddy paces in front of the window, looking out at the snow still falling. He brings one arm up and rubs the back of his neck as he says, "Not a chance your car can get through right now. Hopefully they get a plow out here soon."

"What'd you do today?" Stella asks.

"Umm . . ." I'm distracted. It's not easy, trying to eavesdrop on Teddy, and carry on a conversation with Stella. "We baked cookies and then got a tree." I move the phone, so she can see the tree sitting in the living room.

My twin smiles. "Sounds fun."

Felix says something to her, and she looks away from the phone.

"Looks like we're staying put until the snow stops."

"Really?"

"Felix doesn't think his car will make it."

"Who buys a front-wheel drive car?" I ask loud enough that hopefully he can hear me.

"Everyone in Arizona," Stella says. "On the plus side, skiing will be awesome tomorrow."

"If you manage to get here," I mumble.

"Oh, cheer up, Hol. Sometimes you have to make the most with the cards you're dealt."

"Did you read that in a fortune cookie?"

"Made it up. Just now." Her eyes widen. "Go have *fun*. I'll check in later."

"Bye, Stell."

She kisses the phone and then ends the call.

The awkwardness that I feared all day sets in as the snow piles up. I lose all hope that my siblings are going to make it back when I check the weather app on my phone, and it says the snow is supposed to continue all night long.

My stomach is uneasy, but it rumbles for food.

"Hungry?" I ask Teddy.

He nods. "Always."

"I'll make dinner."

"I can help."

"No, no," I say too quickly. I need a minute without him so close. My nerves are on edge. I plaster on a smile. "I know how you feel about cooking. I've got this."

I open the fridge. Stella and I bought what we thought was enough groceries for the entire weekend, but after sharing with the guys, it's dwindling fast.

"Turkey sandwiches?"

"Yeah, that sounds good."

I pull out everything I need and make us dinner while Teddy puts on a movie—*Jingle All the Way* again, and his laughter at the cheesy holiday movie does funny things to my insides.

"Thanks," he says when I hand him a plate with the sandwich and some chips.

"Welcome." I eat standing up in the kitchen.

Between bites, I find the string of LED lights from my dorm

room I brought to hang on the tree, and it looks even better than I imagined. I only wish I had two or three more strands. After that, I pull out everything to decorate the cookies.

Teddy sits on a stool in front of me, his body angled so he can watch the TV.

I watch him. He finishes his first sandwich in four large bites, then moves on to the chips. I've barely touched my food when he's finished. I take my sandwich and push my plate of chips toward him.

"Thanks."

"We're almost out of food, but we have lots of cookies." I hold one up. He snatches it from me and pops it in his mouth.

"Good," he mumbles as he chews.

I give him a playful glare and smack his hand as he goes in for another cookie. I do a super-fast decorating job on a small bell-shaped cookie and hand it to him. "Sugar cookies without frosting are sad. It's like unfrosted Pop-Tarts. What's the point?"

He laughs, but after he takes the first bite, he nods. "Damn, that's good."

He shoves the rest of it in his mouth and then gets up and pulls a beer out of the fridge.

"That seems like a truly terrible combination," I say, pointing between the two.

"You're right." He sets the beer back and then grabs the RumChata off the top of the fridge. "Cookies and cream."

"If I didn't know better, I'd say you have a sweet tooth."

He fills a coffee mug with the sweet liqueur and downs it. His face twists up. "That's too sweet, even for me."

He reclaims his beer from the fridge.

Together, we decorate the cookies. Well, I decorate, and Teddy eats them. I do my best on the Santa with the small third leg, but it ends up looking like he's packing some serious heat in his trousers.

Teddy politely doesn't mention it, but I notice he doesn't eat that one, either.

By the time we're finished, we've only killed thirty minutes. It's still snowing out. A freaking blizzard. Just what I wanted, but not exactly how I wanted it.

"I don't think they're coming back tonight." A weight settles in my stomach.

"Nope." He gives me an apologetic smile. "Do you want to watch another movie or something?"

I nod. "Yeah. Might as well."

Teddy takes two more cookies and his beer and heads to the living room. I no sooner than step out of the kitchen when the lights flicker. We both freeze. They go out, come back on, and then go out again and stay that way.

Chapter Seven

AN EERIE QUIET STRETCHES BETWEEN US AS WE WAIT for the power to return. The Christmas tree with its small strand of battery-powered lights is the only thing still on.

Teddy goes to the window and looks out. "Neighbor's house is dark, too. Do you have a flashlight or some candles?"

It's not quite sunset outside and Teddy's big frame is lit up as he stands with his back to the window, facing me. That's when it sets in. I mean really sets in. I'm snowed in with Teddy. Freaking snowed in. Just the two of us. With no power.

"Holly?" The way he says my name, rough but somehow soft, snatches my attention.

When I meet his gaze, his gray eyes (though I can't actually make out the color in the dim light) seek me out with concern and care. "We'll be okay."

How do I tell him that my concern isn't that we'll freeze to death but that I might say or do something idiotic and embarrass myself in front of him? This crush feels like it's going to die a cold, humiliating death.

Once you make a big enough ass out of yourself in front of someone you like, you realize that there is absolutely no coming back from it. That's it. The heart moves on. No, not the heart. The brain. It must be a survival technique. When all hope is finally lost, your brain stops sending dopamine or endorphins or whatever it is (science is clearly not my strong suit) that makes your body sing when the other person is around.

I don't want to be over Teddy. This crush feels good, even if I am way, way out of my depth here.

This is one of those instances when I wish I were more like Stella. She would have no problem being snowed in with her crush. But I'm me, and Teddy is still staring at me like I'm about to break down in front of him.

"Lights," I say finally. "I think there might be a flashlight in the master closet, and I saw some candles under the sink."

He moves into action, but I'm slower. He gets close, and I realize I'm in his path and start to move, but he's already going around me and now I'm in front of him again.

"Sorry," I squeak as he braces himself on my shoulders to keep from plowing me over. His chest brushes against mine and I get a whiff of his soap mixed with fir tree.

We both start to move again, but this time, we go in opposite directions.

I grab the candles under the sink and then search the other rooms, finding two more. When I get back to the main room, Teddy has a small flashlight and matches.

He turns the flashlight on and shines it around the dark room, then turns it back off and sets it on the counter. "These were in there too." He holds up the matches.

"Should we save them?"

He shakes his head. "Maybe one, but I doubt the power will be out that long."

We light the candles, leaving one on the kitchen counter, and I bring the others into the living room.

"Well." He blows out a breath and sits on the couch with his beer. "Not a lot we can do now but wait."

"We could put on a movie," I suggest and then immediately chastise myself. "But we don't have any power."

He laughs softly. "Would have been a great idea."

"I have my laptop. We could watch something on that."

"We should probably save it."

I nod, glancing outside. The sky is getting darker, and the snow is still falling. "For emergencies? In case we need to . . . email someone or something."

One side of his mouth lifts and I get a half-dimpled smile. "I meant in case we got bored later."

"Oh, right." I move into the kitchen and pour myself a glass of the RumChata.

"Who would we email, out of curiosity?" Teddy asks when I get back. I sit next to him on the couch. His presence feels even bigger in the near dark.

"I don't know," I say with an embarrassed giggle. "Maybe the power company?"

"Or a snowplow?" he teases.

"So maybe email isn't the best way to contact someone in an emergency, but maybe as a last resort? At least I could email my parents to say goodbye." The room is starting to cool off without the heat on. There's a fireplace but only two logs of firewood because it has always been more about ambience than survival.

Teddy angles his body toward me and places one arm on the back of the couch. "That's sweet."

"Sweet? I just need them to know this is all Felix's fault."

He laughs. I really love Teddy's laugh. It's deep and uninhibited, louder than he is any other time. I take a sip of the drink. It's sweet, but the liqueur heats my throat as I swallow.

"Who would you email?" I ask. "Your dad?"

"First off, we're fine. No one is dying tonight." He winks. "But if I were in a near-death situation, I'd probably try to get ahold of my little brother."

I smile because it's such a fitting answer for Teddy. "How old is he?"

"Seventeen."

"Does he play football?"

"Yeah, but he's a QB like your brother."

"Uh-oh, Felix better watch his back."

Teddy laughs again, this time quieter. "He's pretty good. I don't know if he's going to play college or not. He's already had a lot of offers, including one from Valley U, but he can't stop partying and hooking up long enough to pass his classes."

"Anyone else you would email? A girlfriend, perhaps?" I feel braver the more I sip my drink, which is half-gone I now realize.

"Girlfriend?" One brow quirks up.

I pull my feet up underneath me and lean closer. "I don't know. You could have one."

"You know I don't."

A blush warms my face. I do know that, but I'm happy to hear him say it anyway. "Why not? You're one of the good ones. Hot and nice. I see the way girls look at you."

"How do they look at me?" He seems to genuinely not know that every girl on campus wants him.

"Like they want to tear your clothes off and climb you." He's so big with all those muscles to explore. My insides are on fire as my words hang between us.

Teddy clears his throat. "I don't know what that looks like, but I'm pretty sure the girls I like aren't looking at me like that."

I want to ask what kind of girls he likes because I don't know what his type is, but I'm not quite that brave yet. So instead, I say, "It's something Stella said the other day, but she isn't wrong. You're a great guy, Teddy."

He smiles at me, both of those dimples popping out. "You're pretty great too."

Chapter Eight

AN HOUR PASSES WITHOUT POWER. A NEIGHBOR CAME by to check in on us and tells us the entire street is out. He called the power company (something I should have thought to do) and apparently, the storm knocked down a power line. In other words, we're in for a long night.

But he brought some wood when he saw our pitiful stack, and we now have a roaring fire to keep the main room warm.

Teddy and I settle in front of it on the couch with the plate of cookies and the bottle of RumChata. With the fire going and the lights on the tree, it feels intimate and fun. The alcohol is definitely helping. My insides are now warm and tingly and the initial awkwardness of being snowed in with my crush is gone.

"Do you want to watch a movie now?" Teddy asks.

"Reached peak boredom and no longer care about saving battery to send our final farewells?" I ask with sass I didn't realize I was capable of.

"I saw some paper in the kitchen, you can write on that if it comes to it."

"Okay, but if I don't get to say goodbye to my parents and blame this all on Felix, then I'm going to haunt you in the next life," I say as I get up to grab my laptop from the other room.

"That doesn't sound so bad," he calls.

I open the computer as I walk back. The battery is at 89%, plenty of juice to watch a movie or two. But the thing is, I don't want to watch a movie. Not now. We're talking and I finally don't feel like such a bumbling mess.

"I must not have plugged this in," I say, skirting the truth. "It isn't fully charged."

"Bummer."

I snap the lid closed and set it on the counter. "Want to play a game?"

Two hours and many games of Gin Rummy later, I am more than a little tipsy.

"Your turn to shuffle. I'll be right back," I say as I stand from the couch and my legs wobble.

Teddy eyes me carefully as I steady myself. "You should eat something."

"I'm fine." I use my phone as a flashlight in the bathroom. After I'm finished, I wash my hands and then text Stella to let her know the power is out, but we're okay.

Her response is immediate, and I'd put good money on it being because she was texting Beau. *You're snowed in with Teddy AND the lights are out?!* She then proceeds to add a bunch of emojis—snow, house, hearts, an eggplant.

I start to tell her it isn't like that, but maybe it can be? I'm aware it's likely the alcohol talking, but I let myself believe it anyway. At least we're having fun and I'm actually talking to him.

Teddy is looking at his phone when I return. He slides it into his pocket and sits forward. I grab a cookie from the plate. The Santa one with a bulge, as chance would have it.

"You gave Santa a third leg," I say, holding it up.

Teddy's cheeks go pink. "I shouldn't be allowed in the kitchen."

I take a bite of Santa's head and Teddy watches intently, his pupils widening. He clears his throat and picks up the cards. "Another game?"

While we play, I munch on cookies and pay more attention to Teddy than the cards in my hand. He smiles at me, playful and flirty, and more than once, his stare drops to my mouth.

"Do you want another drink?" I ask as I fill my glass again. All those cookies made me thirsty.

He hesitates. "That depends. How are you feeling?"

"What?"

"I want to be able to take care of you if you get sick." He rubs the back of his neck like he's embarrassed to have said it out loud. *Ugh.* That's totally something a big brother would think and not a guy hoping to see you naked.

"I'm fine. I think the sugar helped." I stand up and proceed to walk in a straight line, arms out. The movement lifts my sweater above my belly button, and Teddy's gaze drops to my bare skin. "See? I'm fine."

His throat works with a swallow. His voice is like gravel when he says, "Yeah, I'll have another drink."

The way he watches me makes me feel powerful, or maybe that's the alcohol talking. I start for the kitchen, but he says, "I can get it."

He grabs two beers, opens one and takes a long drink. Then his eyes are on me again. My heart beats so loudly, I'm sure he can hear it. It feels like an invisible line is tugging us together, but he doesn't budge.

Stella's words echo in my head. *You have to make a move because he never will.*

I don't know how Teddy feels about me. These heated looks are in direct contradiction to his actions, but maybe Stella is right. Is it possible he has noticed me the way I notice him? That he sees me as more than Felix's little sister?

I go to him before I come up with an answer. His brows tug together in confusion at my nearness, but it doesn't stop me. My courage is a living, breathing thing propelling me forward. Lifting up on my toes, I kiss him. His lips are soft and warm. He tastes like sugar and beer, and I know I said it was a terrible combination, but I was so wrong.

My hands rest on his chest and I lean into him, so our entire upper bodies are mashed together. My body vibrates. It is everything I hoped it would be.

I'm so into it that it takes me a moment to realize that he is *not* into it. His immovable lips underneath mine sober me up instantly. I freeze, hoping he'll take over or come to his senses. He doesn't.

I step back, hand flying to cover my mouth, like I can erase that kiss by wiping away the evidence from my lips.

Oh god. What have I done? *What have I freaking done?!*

Chapter Nine

TEDDY'S EXPRESSION IS IMPOSSIBLE TO READ. SHOCKED? Horrified? Stunned?

I move backward, fingers still covering my tingling lips.

"I'm sorry. The dim lighting, the alcohol, plus I think I have a sugar high . . ." I release a shaky breath. "I'm going to bed. See you in the morning, Teddy."

The back of my eyes sting as I move through the dark house to the room Stella and I have been sleeping in. When I throw open the door and step inside, it's freezing. *Holy crap.*

My phone is still out in the living room, so I rummage around in the dark to find a sweatshirt. Even after I pulled on the extra layer, I'm still so cold.

Lying on the bed, I stare up at the ceiling. This cabin is so small, I can hear Teddy moving around in the other room.

Why did I have to kiss him? I fling my arm over my eyes, which incidentally provides a little extra warmth to my cold face. If I get any sleep tonight, it will be a small miracle.

I'm never going to be able to look him in the eye again. *Groan.*

I wish I could text Stella. She always knows what to say or do when it comes to guys.

Teddy must have stopped moving around because when he starts again, I'm acutely aware of it. His steps get closer and then there's a knock at my door. I sit up, heart racing. My voice is caught in my throat.

"Holly?" Teddy's deep voice is gentle. He doesn't strike me as the kind of guy who would want to have a heart-to-heart after I jumped him and made an ass out of myself. Can't he let a girl lick her wounds in private?

"Yeah?" My voice shakes, but I'm not sure if it's the cold or my nerves.

The door opens a crack and Teddy finds me with the flash-light, then moves it, so it's not blinding me. This time, when he speaks, his voice has a hard edge. "It's freezing in here."

I pull at the sleeves of my sweatshirt. "My dad is always say-ing the place needs new windows."

I can't believe I just kissed him and we're talking about windows.

He pushes the door wide, steps to the bed and takes the com-forter. "Bring your pillow."

Scrambling from bed, I follow in a haze of embarrassment and confusion. He sets the flashlight on the counter, tosses the comforter in the master bedroom then takes my pillow and tosses it too.

"O-kay." I start for the room, but Teddy grabs hold of my arm.

"Wait." He lets go and then brings his palms together, rub-bing them lightly.

"Whatever you're going to say, can you not?"

His gray eyes narrow as he studies me.

"I shouldn't have done that. Kiss you, I mean. I didn't mean it." The lie burns my tongue. "It was silly. I thought it would be funny, like a joke. And then it wasn't."

Not funny at all.

"Are you drunk?"

"What? No," I say quickly, and then add, "maybe a little."

"Did you kiss me because you're drunk?"

The more he presses me, the more frustrated I become. "No,

I've thought about it for a long time, all right? Now, if you'll excuse me, I'm going to bed and sleeping until I forget this night happened."

He steps into my path. "Here's the thing, Holly."

I take a tentative step back. Something in his voice, his demeanor, makes the hair on the back of my neck prickle.

"We can pretend that didn't happen. That it was a joke or a spontaneous, meaningless mistake. I can do that. I'll never say a word about it to anyone."

My heart tears down the middle at how badly I've screwed this up. Maybe he can forget that easily, but I cannot.

He erases the space between us. "*Or*, we can try again. Your call."

My heart picks up speed and my mind spins. "Try again?"

He lets out a rough chuckle and his dimples appear in a cocky smile. "You caught me off guard. I wasn't expecting it and I was a little worried you were doing something you didn't mean because of the alcohol. Under different circumstances, I would have kissed you a whole lot better than I did."

"You didn't kiss me at all."

His smile slips into a smirk. "Then let me have another shot."

I dip my chin, giving him permission, and that's all the encouragement Teddy needs. Both of his rough palms frame my face and his mouth slants over mine. His touch is gentle, but his kiss is not.

I melt into him, letting him take control, and just savor it. When his tongue seeks entrance, I open wider for him. He's tall, leaning down to reach my mouth, but when I move my hands around his neck, he stands a little straighter and pulls me up to him.

The movement presses our bodies flush and Teddy groans. I can't believe I'm responsible for that noise, but it makes me bolder.

I curl my fingers in the thick hair at the nape of his neck and kiss him like I've always wanted to. If tonight, this moment, is it, I don't want to have any regrets.

Still kissing, we move to the couch. Teddy sits down and brings me onto his lap. He's hard underneath me, so very hard.

I get another delicious groan out of him as I roll my hips. I've never been particularly bold when it comes to sex. For me, getting intimate with someone requires a level of trust and vulnerability I haven't felt with a lot of guys. And even with those I have slept with, I've let them make the first move, taking my cues from there, but Teddy is so responsive to my every touch that it makes me want to explore and catalog his every reaction.

When I sigh into his mouth, his kisses get harder. When I scrape my nails lightly down his shoulders, he nips at my lower lip. And when I can't take it anymore and let my head fall back in pure bliss, he presses soft open-mouth kisses along the column of my neck.

The fire crackles behind me and when I lift my head, Teddy's gaze burns into mine.

"You can have the bed. I'll sleep out here," he murmurs, but then brushes another soft kiss on my lips.

"Who's sleeping?" My fingers dance along the hem of his shirt and slip under to his warm skin.

His rough chuckle does nothing to deter me, but Teddy takes my hands in his. "We don't need to rush this. I don't want you to do anything you'll regret tomorrow."

I could never regret him, even if it blew up in my face. Hide forever? Yes. But never regret.

I bring my mouth to his and rest my lips lightly against his. "I feel like if I stop kissing you, you're going to disappear or I'm going to wake up tomorrow and it'll all have been a dream."

He pulls my bottom lip between his teeth and tugs gently. "I'm not going anywhere."

I stand, taking his hand and giving it a tug. "Except to bed with me."

He resists, giving me a conflicted look. "To sleep. And maybe make out a tiny bit more." I bring my free hand up and show him with my thumb and pointer finger. "You can't possibly want to sleep on this couch another night."

"It's not so bad."

"Theodore."

His laugh is silent, but it twinkles in his eyes. "I like it when you say my name."

I take a step back. "Theodore."

"You always call me Teddy." His mouth twitches.

Another step. I take off one of my sweatshirts and toss it at him. "Teddy, will you please share your body heat with me tonight?"

He gets to his feet, and I walk backward, so I can keep staring and smiling at him. I can't freaking stop smiling.

"Anything you want, *Holly*." He makes a point to say my name in a deep, rough voice that is intentionally meant to taunt me the same way I'm doing to him.

He doesn't know yet that everything he does drives me crazy.

Chapter Ten

I climb into bed and Teddy kicks off his shoes and then gets in beside me.

Rolling to my side, I fist his shirt and move closer. He might have been hesitant about following me in here, but there is absolutely nothing tentative about the way he kisses me.

It's a high so far beyond alcohol or the one-time Stella convinced me to try an edible. Kissing Teddy is like being on the spinning teacups while drunk and laughing hysterically.

We kiss until my lips hurt. My cheeks hurt too, from smiling. I'm giddy.

Lying on our sides, we stare at each other. Teddy's hand rests on my hip, and he traces little circles with his thumb. I'm playing with the strings on his hoodie, wrapping them around my fingers and occasionally using them as leverage to pull him closer for more kisses.

"You have a devious glint in your eye. What are you thinking about?" he asks.

"You. Me. How we spent the past hour sucking face. I still can't believe it's really happening." I lean forward and kiss him again. "I've wanted to do that for so long."

"Me too."

"You have not."

"I swear it. Ever since last year. You came downstairs on Christmas Eve wearing your little reindeer onesie. I was feeling sorry for myself, missing my family, thinking about my mom, and you just sat and talked with me. I don't even remember what about."

"Reindeer names."

"What?"

"You called me Rudolph and I said I didn't have a red nose, so we went through Santa's other reindeer's names, but you said none of those fit, so we tried to come up with others." I'm certain my face is red with embarrassment. I'd forgotten about that conversation. "You make me nervous and I say the dumbest things."

"It wasn't dumb. You were cute. I love listening to you talk."

I shake my head in disbelief.

"I thought you were cute before then, but Felix is your brother, so I did my best not to think of you as anything but a friend. But that night, you were there for me in a way no one had been in a long time."

"What do you mean? I see girls hitting on you all the time."

"Yeah, sure, but they don't know me. Or even want to. Their intentions are shallow and I'm not into that." One shoulder lifts in a small shrug. "After my mom died, I don't know, I have a lower tolerance for superficial relationships, I guess."

"I'm sorry you lost her so young."

He nods. "Me too. I hate it more for my brother. He hardly remembers her."

"Will you tell me about her?"

"What do you want to know?"

I move closer. "Everything."

His lips slant over mine in a quick kiss and then he does.

Teddy and I stay up talking most of the night. About his mom, his dad and brother, about football. He asks me stuff too, about being a twin, about my first semester at Valley. I don't think I've stayed up all night talking to anyone else this way, except Stella.

We leave the bedroom door open so that some of the warmth from the fire seeps in. Even so, we really do need to snuggle for warmth.

When I wake up, Teddy is on his back, and I'm curled up on my side with my head on his shoulder. I glance up and see his eyes open.

"Morning." His voice is deep and rough with sleep.

"Hi."

"Power came back on."

I sit up and look out the window. The sun is shining, and the house is warm. "Have you heard from Felix?"

"They're on their way back."

Something like disappointment washes over me. Teddy must read my expression because he says, "Come here."

I drop onto his chest, and he kisses me, slow and tender at first, but we both know our time alone together is limited and each kiss grows more frantic. He's hard beneath me and my body trembles with every brush of him against my core.

He has a tight grip on my hips and starts to move me over his length, as he thrusts up to provide more friction.

I briefly wish there were fewer clothes between us, but honestly, the way my body soars, it'd probably be over far sooner than I want if we were naked.

When his hands finally move, it's under my sweatshirt to cup my breasts. He groans. "So perfect."

He lifts up to press kisses to the top of my cleavage over my bra, then falls back and presses harder into me.

"Do you want to take these off?" I hook a finger in the waistband of his sweatpants.

"No time for that."

I stop, thinking he means there's no time to keep going, but he reclaims control of my body, placing those big hands on either hip, doing the work for me. I'm feverish with need as my orgasm hangs just beyond my grasp.

"Come for me, sweetheart."

Sweetheart. A word I never imagined Teddy using for me. It does the trick, sending me over the edge in a swirl of emotional and physical climax.

As the last of my orgasm falls away, Teddy's hands still on my hips.

"Wha—" Before I can finish the sentence, I hear a car door shut outside.

I scramble off Teddy. He's slower to get up but swings his legs over the side of the bed and runs a hand over his bedhead.

My gaze goes to the massive erection tenting his sweatpants. "How are you going to hide that?"

"Shower." He winks and then disappears. The water comes on a second later. I adjust my clothes and finger-comb my hair. I'm rushing into the living room as they enter the house.

Stella gives me a knowing smirk, Lucas nods and heads straight for the fridge, Emmett plops down on the couch, but Felix comes up short and his gaze narrows. "Hey. What's up? You look weird."

Your best friend just gave me the best orgasm of my life, fully clothed at that. Obviously, I don't say that. Instead, I stick my tongue out at him. "*You* look weird."

"Long drive." He runs a hand through his hair. "Roads are still pretty icy close to the cabin. What time did the power come back on last night?"

"Uhhh . . ."

"And where's Teddy?" He looks around.

"Shower." Probably taking care of himself. My face is so hot. I duck my head and pick up the mess from last night in the living room while Felix heads toward his room.

"Wait," I call at the last second, remembering my stuff is in there. "I left a few things."

I rush past him and get my comforter and pillow. Both smell faintly of Teddy and I breathe him in.

"Gross." Felix scrunches up his nose. "You slept in my bed."

I roll my eyes. "The other room was freezing without the heat on."

"Why is Teddy's shirt in here?" He picks it up from the end of the bed, where one of us tossed it mid-makeout.

"I don't know." The words come out squeaky and defensive. "He must have taken it off before he got in the shower."

Felix stares at me a beat before he says, "Okay. I'm going to change and then let's go check out the slopes." He waggles his brows. "Fresh powder."

Chapter Eleven

E VERYONE HAS THE SAME IDEA WE DID ABOUT ENJOYING the fresh snow. I promised Stella I would ski with her, so I dutifully strap on my gear, and we head for the bunny hill.

She peppers me with questions about last night, but it's all I can do to stay upright, and talking about kissing Teddy is a major distraction.

"Stell, can we talk about this later?"

She sighs, loudly. "Fine. You're doing that all wrong. You have to make the wedge, like a pizza, remember?"

"I'm trying."

"Here." She moves in front of me to help guide me in position.

Thirty minutes and several trips down the hill later, I'm finally ready to get on the lift.

"I need to pee first," Stella says.

"Now?" I laugh.

"I had like a gallon of coffee on the trip back." We move over to the food hut next to the skating rink. There are bathrooms inside, so you don't have to trek all the way back inside the resort in times like these. She takes off her skis and then hands me her poles. "Be right back."

While I wait, I watch families skating together. Dads holding on to their little ones and pulling them along; kids with skating aids marching around with huge grins on their faces.

There is holiday music playing over the outdoor speakers and the air has a festive feel with all the happy laughter and smiles of pure joy. All of it makes me miss my parents. I hope they're having fun and I can't wait to see them and cram all the holiday traditions we can into the rest of the school break.

"Yo, Holly!"

I turn at my name to find Felix, Emmett, and Lucas skiing over to me. Teddy is behind them. His cheeks are red, and one side of his pants is covered in snow.

"Been out yet?" my brother asks.

"No. We were just about to go." I tip my head to the hut. "Stella had to use the bathroom. What are you guys doing back so soon?"

"Snack break," Felix says.

"And Teddy needs to warm up." Lucas snickers.

I fight a smile. "I want to laugh, but I have a feeling I'm going to be in the same position as soon as I get up there."

The rest of the guys take off their gear and head inside, but Teddy lingers. He has a blue hat that matches his coat pulled low over his ears, but the ends of his hair curl around the back.

"I'm pretty sure I broke my tailbone." He winces as he rubs the side of his butt.

"That's not where your tailbone is."

He glances over to where Felix and Lucas disappeared before kissing me. We didn't have time this morning to talk about what last night meant or if we're going to keep doing it.

"Stella knows about us," I tell him when he pulls back. "Not everything, but she's always known how I felt."

He nods. "I figured."

"What about Felix?"

"I'll tell him," he says, "I haven't had time today, but I will tell him. I owe him that."

"We should do it together. I don't want you to feel like you have to ask permission. This is between us."

Except I don't really know what *this* is, but he kisses me again, so I guess it involves kissing, and I'm good with that.

We ski all day, then go back to the cabin long enough to shower and change. Emmett had to leave to get home for the holidays, but the rest of us head back to the resort for a night out. We get a big corner booth in the restaurant. Stella is on one side of me, Teddy the other.

We order a bunch of appetizers to share, and the mood is fun and light. Felix and Lucas are teasing Teddy about falling down the mountain today. My brother has this huge grin on his face as he tells us how his feet were over his head and Teddy looked like Sonic the Hedgehog in a cloud of blue rolling down the hill, snow flying everywhere.

Teddy lifts his glass to his lips with one hand, but the other finds my bare thigh under the table. I thought this skirt was a good idea. It's red and green flannel, short. Very holiday but still sexy. And I paired it with my favorite over-the-knee boots. I did not imagine this happening, though.

I make a squeak of surprise, which I cover with a cough. Stella drops her stare to my lap and then giggles into her napkin. Thankfully, no one else looks twice.

Teddy chuckles quietly and lets his fingers graze higher. I squeeze my legs together, but now his hand is trapped between my thighs. Two inches higher and he could feel how wet he's making me.

Which sounds nice and I could be into him having his hand up my skirt in public under different circumstances, but not with my brother across the table.

I set my napkin on the table and scoot closer to Stella. "Come with me to the bar."

"Why?" she asks, lips twisting in amusement. "Something wrong?"

"You got a fake ID I don't know about?" Felix asks.

"No. I want to see if they'll make me one of those holiday drinks, the Christmas mimosa, but you know, virgin."

Teddy was taking a drink and now shoots the liquid out of his mouth as he starts coughing.

"Sorry," he says, voice tight. "Wrong tube."

My face burns. I shoot him a *get your head out of the gutter before my brother figures us out* glare and then I push against Stella, forcing her to move.

"Okay, okay. Let a girl get her shoes on." She stumbles as she slides into the stilettos she'd taken off while we were seated.

"Our server is coming. You can order it from him," Felix calls behind us. I don't look back, but I'm sure Teddy is laughing.

"I don't know how you wear these." Stella winces as she walks.

"Practice."

"Hmm." She hums. "I need more of it because those boots are amazing." She gives me a once-over and then her lips quirk up at the corners. "Teddy seems to have noticed as well. You guys are cute."

I blow out a breath as we squeeze into an open spot at the bar. "Yeah, well, I have two years of pent-up sexual frustration. I'm going to combust."

"Should have followed him into that shower this morning."

I finally told Stella everything while we were getting ready for dinner. She was appropriately excited for me, but telling someone just made it all feel so much more real, and now I am dying to tell Felix, so we can stop sneaking around.

Is he going to freak out? I don't think so, but I'm worried his reaction will change how Teddy sees me.

"He's looking over here," Stella says, leaning one elbow on the bar top.

I peek over my shoulder to meet Teddy's playful stare. Lucas says something, pulling his attention away, but his gaze returns a second later.

"I can't handle any more teasing." I fidget, trying to calm the buzz skating over my skin and pulsing in my core.

"You know what you need?"

"Yes. A six-foot-two football player with fingers like magic and a kiss that makes my knees weak."

"Daaaang." Stella laughs lightly. "You have it bad."

"So bad. I didn't think it was possible to like him more. What am I going to do?"

"I have an idea."

"It was a rhetorical question. We're going to tell Felix and then we won't have to steal kisses and touches when no one is looking."

"I think you should lean in. Have a sexy, little holiday vacation fling. You can tell Felix after we leave. And I have the perfect way for you to dish out a little teasing of your own." She lifts a brochure from the bar and holds it up. "The resort is having their annual party. A very fancy party, where we can get all dolled up and dance under the twinkle lights. Teddy will eat his heart out seeing you all done up and not being able to touch you."

Stella holds her arms out and looks up at the ceiling. "How fun would that be? I've always wanted to go, but we've never been here during the party."

My phone buzzes in my purse. I pull it out and get a little zap of excitement when I see Teddy's name.

"Theodore?" Stella asks.

"Yeah."

I show her the screen, *You can't hide from me forever, sweetheart.*

Laughing, Stella says, "He is a tease. I so love this for you. Playful and sexy."

A wistful look crosses her face.

"You should invite Beau."

"He's busy with his family."

"Bummer."

"Yeah." She nods her agreement.

I take the brochure. Images of Teddy and I dancing and kissing float through my mind. "What would we even wear to this?"

Her face lights up. "Does that mean we're going?"

I meet Teddy's stare across the room. His eyes darken and his mouth twists into a smirk.

"Absolutely."

Get ready to eat your heart out, Teddy.

Chapter Twelve

"**Y**OU'RE NOT COMING?" TEDDY ASKS THE NEXT morning when everyone else is getting ready to head to the resort. Today they're snowboarding and Stella is next-level excited.

I shake my head. "Nope. I am going to go shopping for a few last-minute gifts and then get more groceries. Someone ate all the food. Even the cookies."

"Can you pick up some more mixers?" Felix asks, shrugging on his coat. "Garrison and James are coming up tonight."

"Wait, you guys are partying here tonight? Stella and I were going to finally do our holiday movie marathon and make gingerbread houses."

"Tonight? Why can't you do that when we get back home?"

"You know Mom will be in a tailspin, trying to get everything ready. The only thing the three of us are going to be doing Christmas Eve is helping her."

He shrugs. "I can try to get everyone outside or in the living room, so you can have the kitchen."

Except everyone will be trekking in and out for booze. I sigh. "I guess we'll do it tomorrow before the dance. Are you guys going to that?"

"You know it." He slaps Teddy in the arm with the back of his hand. "I even convinced this one."

My brows rise and my gaze slides to Teddy. "Did you?"

"Everyone else is going. I figured I might as well." His lips twitch with amusement. I convinced him, thank you very much.

"All right." Felix claps his gloved hands. "Let's roll out."

"Bye!" Stella calls with a smile, quickly following after Felix. Lucas leaves too, but Teddy lingers.

"Sorry about tonight."

"It's okay. I knew when we pulled up and Felix was half-naked and wearing his Santa hat that this vacation was not going to go like I planned. I just miss it, you know? All the silly things we do every year."

A hint of understanding crosses his face.

"It's stupid. Here I am feeling sorry for myself because things aren't going perfectly, and you aren't even going to see your family for Christmas."

"You can still be disappointed. It's important to you. Anything I can do?" He inches forward until his pinky finger curls around mine.

"I'm good," I say. And I am. Better than good, in fact.

After everyone is gone, I go to a few stores. I still need to get Stella a Christmas gift, but I don't find anything for her. She's so good at picking things out for me, but I struggle with her. She always just steals my stuff anyway, which is how I talk myself into buying the new pair of shoes I find. They'll look great with the dress I plan to wear to the dance tomorrow night. I also pick up mixers for Felix, some more groceries to hold us over until we leave, and enough cookie dough and icing to decorate a thousand more cookies.

I put on *Christmas Vacation*, which makes me miss my dad even more (he's a total Clark Griswold with the crazy amount of lights he puts on our house every year), and I bake cookies.

I am pulling the last batch out of the oven when the front

door of the cabin opens and Stella steps inside. Her cheeks and nose are rosy, and her hair is pulled back in a windblown ponytail. She smiles as she says, "It smells so good in here."

Felix is the next through the door. "Holly!"

Teddy and Lucas are behind him. They all peel out of their coats and outerwear. Felix snatches a cookie from the cooling rack.

Smacking at his hand, I say, "They aren't decorated yet."

"So?"

Teddy steps forward and grabs one, takes a bite, and then looks at me as he says, "It's like eating an unfrosted Pop-Tart."

"Which is still delicious," Felix says seriously.

I grab a plate and set it on the counter. "These are the broken ones. Eat these."

"We got something for you too." My brother lifts a sack onto the counter.

"For me?"

I dig in while Felix explains, "I feel bad that you and Stella planned this whole trip and I sort of ruined it."

"You feel bad?" I question. "Who are you and what have you done with my brother?"

One side of his mouth pulls up. "Ha, ha."

I pull out a wad of red material and unfold it in front of me. It's a holiday sweater. A really, *really* ugly one. It has a cat knitting a stocking with the ski resort logo.

"I don't know what to say." I look hesitantly from Felix to Stella.

They both bust up laughing.

"We all got them." Stella lifts the bag in her hand and takes out another sweater, somehow even more hideous than mine.

One by one, they each show me their sweaters, all equally hideous.

"These are truly awful," I say. "Why would you buy these?"

"An ugly holiday sweater party!" Stella beams.

"Wait, really? Tonight?" Excitement bubbles up inside me.

"It was Teddy's idea." Felix lays his sweatshirt over one shoulder.

"This was your idea?" I quickly glance at Teddy, who gives me a sheepish smile, and the tips of his ears turn a slight pink.

"We got booze and mixers to make those Christmas mimosas you like and . . ." Felix grins wide while he digs inside another bag and pulls out a box of Jolly Rancher candy canes—my favorite. "Merry Christmas, Holl."

I take the box and then hug him with my free arm. "Thank you."

"I call shower first," Lucas says. "Wait until you see me in this sexy snowman sweater, Stella."

He does a little dance, holding up the sweater in front of him.

"I'm Holly, you idiot," she says.

"Wait, what?" He looks between us and everyone else laughs.

"Don't do that to me. I think I finally got it." Lucas shakes his head and disappears into the bathroom.

Felix unpacks the booze and throws in a couple of frozen pizzas for dinner, while Stella showers in the other bathroom.

It's just me, Teddy, and Felix, and I make eye contact with Teddy and mouth, "Should we tell him now?"

Teddy shakes his head and mouths something back, but I can't make sense of it. It doesn't matter though, because Lucas takes the world's fastest shower and reappears a minute later, dark hair still wet, but wearing jeans and his snowman sweater. He looks ridiculous.

"You want next shower?" Felix asks Teddy.

"Nah, go ahead."

"Are you sure? Might not be a lot of hot water left after I'm done."

Teddy chuckles, but says, "Go ahead. I want to text my brother and dad."

Felix nods and shuts the door behind him as he goes into the master bedroom.

Teddy moves closer to me in the kitchen, takes another cookie, and whispers, "Sorry. I do want to tell him, but you know that girl he hung out with the other night, Tricia?"

"Yeah."

"Well, he's been texting her the past two days to hang out again, and I guess she told him she'd already left, but then today, we saw her with some other guy at the resort."

"Ouch."

"I don't want to rub it in his face when he's down. Let's have fun tonight and we can tell him tomorrow."

"You're a good friend to him." I lift up my sweater. "And this is amazing. How did you talk them into it?"

He rubs at the back of his neck, something I noticed he does when he's uncomfortable. "I may have had to play the, *I'm not going home for Christmas this year* card."

I laugh. "Seriously, thank you."

"Don't thank me yet. You haven't seen what I look like in my *very* festive, very *small* sweater." He holds out the white sweatshirt. It says Merry Christmas in red sequins that turn white when you flip them the other way. And it's about half the width of him. "There weren't any more extra larges."

"Oh, this is going to be amazing," I say.

Chapter Thirteen

THE PARTY IS AMAZING. THE GUYS ARE HILARIOUS IN their sweaters (Lucas cut the sleeves to show off his biceps—which admittedly are nice, but he looks ridiculous), the mimosas are perfection, and Felix has on his Santa hat and demands the TV stay on *Elf* the entire night.

We've just restarted it and are halfway through the second time, which is a lot of Will Ferrell in an elf costume. The guys make a drinking game out of it, picking different words for each other and drinking every time Buddy says their word. Poor Teddy got 'Santa,' and he is *feeling it.*

"You're pretty," he says, when I take a seat next to him on the couch. His eyes are hooded and his sweatshirt is pushed up his forearms because it doesn't come all the way down his long arms. His head falls back, and he keeps staring at me. "My mom would have liked you."

My heart kicks up a notch. "Oh yeah? Because I'm pretty in my holiday kitty sweater?"

He moves his head side to side slowly. "She really loved Christmas. I think it's why my dad doesn't like to celebrate it anymore."

That makes my heart squeeze. I can't imagine.

"But she'd also think you're really pretty. And nice. And pretty. Did I mention you are pretty?"

Stella is on her phone next to me. She looks up long enough to laugh at Teddy. "You mentioned that a few times, Theodore."

"I meant it. I need water." He gets to his feet. The sweater is so small. The bottom hem barely covers his stomach. But, somehow, he still looks sexy.

"Water is good," I tell him. "Maybe a few cookies too. I hear they help for this sort of thing."

He grins. "Hope this night ends like that one."

I know it won't, but the thought of it makes my stomach flip anyway.

"Beau is definitely coming to visit over the break," Stella says, when it's just the two of us left in the living room.

"Really? That's great."

Her body deflates with a breath. "It is great, but I'm nervous. I want it to go well."

"I'm sure we'll all like him, if you do."

"Yeah." She nods, but she doesn't look convinced. "He's so excited to meet you."

"I'm excited too."

"You should invite Teddy. We can go out one night together, the four of us." She gives me a hopeful smile.

"Yeah." I find him in the kitchen guzzling a glass of water. Teddy meets my gaze. His eyes are hazy, but he smiles and those dimples appear, and then he winks at me.

I can't believe this is happening. Me and Teddy, making eyes across the room and planning double dates. It didn't start out how I expected, but I don't want this vacation to end.

The next day, Stella and I spend hours getting ready for the dance. It feels like prom all over again. We try on every dress we brought until she settles on a red one with tiny straps that show off her toned arms and shoulders. She lets me do her makeup but opts for a simple braid for her hair.

I go all out. Big curls, heavier makeup, sexy green dress, and my secret weapon—sexy shoes.

"When did you get those?" Stella stares at the strappy gold shoes with admiration.

"The other day when you guys were snowboarding. Are they too much?"

"No. They are stunning. You are a goddess." She turns to stare at herself in the mirror. "I wish Beau were here. Although, I'd be worried he'd take one look at you and regret meeting me first."

I laugh. "Oh, please."

Her face is marred with insecurity that is so rare to see on my twin's face that it throws me for a loop.

"No way. You are gorgeous and everything is going to go great when he comes to visit."

"Hol, there's something I haven't told you about Beau." She sits on the edge of the bed.

"What?"

"Let's go!" Felix calls from the living room.

I crack open the door and tell him we'll be right there, and then look to my sister.

"Never mind." She stands and her mouth curves up. "Let's do this! I want to see Theodore swallow his tongue when he gets a look at you."

Stella goes out first. I take one more look at myself in the mirror and follow.

The guys are sitting in the living room playing video games. Lucas notices Stella first and then his stare slides to me.

"Woah," he says. His gaze bounces between us. "I don't know which is which, but you both look *super* hot."

Felix smacks him even before he looks away from the screen. "You're talking about my sisters, dude."

"Sorry, but they are."

They continue bickering, but it's background noise because the second that Teddy looks up at me, everything else falls away and it's just the two of us. He stands. I think one of the guys complains that the game isn't over, but Teddy crosses the room to me. He doesn't speak as he takes me in. His hair is styled neatly, but still curls at the ends. The black button-down shirt he's wearing stretches over his broad chest and back.

"Hi," I say quietly.

His throat works with a swallow, but he still doesn't say a word.

Stella giggles and mutters, "Told you so."

Chapter Fourteen

THE SKI RESORT LODGE HAS BEEN TRANSFORMED FOR the party. There are lights strung from the ceiling, and trees decorated in every corner, as the band plays holiday tunes.

People are dancing and standing at the bar. It's an interesting mix of families and couples. I see Tricia and send her a mean glare. The guy that she's with keeps checking out other girls when she's not looking. It's hard to feel sorry for her.

Teddy stays by my side, occasionally brushing his fingers against mine or touching my lower back. I'm never going to survive the night without kissing him. I'm keeping an eye out for a dark corner to shove him into.

Stella is on her phone, texting Beau, I'm sure.

"Put that away," I tell her. "You're missing this and it's incredible."

"Okay, okay." She tucks it into her purse and adjusts the strap of her little Prada crossbody bag. "You're right. I've wanted to go to this party for years."

Lucas spins and holds out his hand to her. "Dance, Stella?"

"Impressive. You can finally tell us apart."

He holds up his hand. Something is scribbled in ink. He stares at his palm as he reads, "Holly is in green, and Stella is in red."

"Oh my gosh." She laughs. "That is truly pathetic." But she slips her hand into his.

"I'm going to the bar," Garrison says. He and James both came back for the party tonight, and so did a few more of their teammates that were close enough to drive up.

"I'll come with you." James looks to Felix. "Walters?"

"Yep." He pops the p and nudges Teddy. "A couple of hot chicks just walked in alone. Let's go talk to them."

Felix takes a step and pauses, waiting for Teddy. An awkward beat passes between them. Oh no. We didn't plan for this. Felix still doesn't know, and of course, he wants his best wingman to troll for girls with him. The thought of Teddy talking to other girls, of them flirting with him and thinking they have a shot of going home with him tonight, makes jealousy course through me.

"No thanks, man." Teddy laces our fingers together and takes a step toward the dance floor.

My pulse races as I watch my brother stare at our joined hands. Felix's dark brows rise, and I can see understanding slowly dawn on his face. "My sister, really?"

Heat trickles up my neck.

Teddy seems completely unfazed. He smiles. "The only hot chick I want to talk to is right here."

Felix makes a gagging sound. "Can everyone stop referring to my baby sisters as hot?"

"Sorry, buddy. Your sister is hot, and I like her." His gray eyes pool with warmth. "A lot."

My stomach is doing somersaults. I step closer to Teddy and squeeze his hand, then wait for Felix's reaction.

"I need a drink. We'll talk about this later, Theodore," he says, but my brother's lips pull into a smile before he heads off to the bar.

"That's one way to tell him," I say as Teddy wraps his arms around my waist.

"Felix is cool," he says.

"He already knew?"

Teddy bobs his head side to side. "Not exactly. I guess last night I must have said something about the girl I was talking to. This morning, the guys were giving me shit and asking me who it was. I actually think Lucas figured it out, because he asked me on the way here if I could put a good word in with Stella."

I glance over where the two of them are dancing. Stella is looking at the doorway.

"He can't even tell us apart." I laugh. "Besides, I think she is off the market." I inch closer and rest my hands around the back of his neck. We sway to the music.

He drops a kiss to my lips. "Too bad for Lucas."

I laugh and rest my head on his shoulder.

He runs a hand down the back of my head, threading his fingers in my hair. "I can't believe I'm dancing with the hottest girl at the party."

Laughing, I smile up at him. "Are you eating your heart out?"

He cocks his head to the side. "What?"

"Nothing." I snuggle into his big chest again. "Nothing at all."

We stay for two more songs before Teddy pulls me off the dance floor. Everyone else is occupied, so we sneak outside and walk around the building to a secluded spot on the property. He wraps his arms around me to keep me warm and we get lost in long, hungry kisses.

He makes a rough, frustrated sound deep in his throat when I reach down and trail my fingers over the bulge in his pants.

I already knew Teddy was built, from the dry-humping session the other night, but I feel a jolt of pleasure at just how fantastic he is. Long and hard, and yes, thick.

He mutters under his breath and groans as I explore. I

stroke him over his clothes, getting more of those sexy noises out of him, but I need more.

His entire body shudders when I press my body into his. "You're killing me, sweetheart."

"Sorry."

"Don't be. I'll die a happy man. Turn around."

I comply, facing the other direction. His hand drops to my thigh and then slowly grazes up and underneath the skirt of my dress. If anyone were to walk out here, we'd look like a happy couple cuddling in the night, but under my dress, Teddy's fingers push my panties to the side and rub small circles over my clit.

"Not fair. I can't reach you." My words are breathy, and goosebumps race up my arms.

Teddy sweeps my hair away from my neck to kiss me. "Just enjoy, sweetheart."

He nudges my legs farther apart. I let my head fall back on his shoulder as his fingers pump in and out of me at a slow, torturous pace.

The Christmas Waltz plays inside, and occasionally happy voices and laughter filter out with the music. I've often felt like I'm on the outside, looking in, but when I'm with Teddy, it's like everyone else is missing out, instead of the other way around.

"Teddy." I gasp as pleasure builds and spikes.

"Sweetheart," he murmurs and sucks hard on the side of my neck.

Spots dance before my vision as I come. Teddy holds me as I sink into him and gulp in air. His dick twitches between us.

I swivel around and peer up at him. "Your turn."

He shakes his head. "We should get back to the party."

"Don't cockblock me, Teddy."

His deep laughter rings out into the night, then he places a quick kiss on my lips and says, "When I come, I want to be inside you, sweetheart."

He lifts our raised hands and places a kiss on my wrist as we walk back.

"How much longer do you think we have to stay?" I ask, anticipation for him being inside me already has my body tingling again.

One side of his mouth lifts. Before he can speak, raised voices grab our attention, and our steps slow as we come around the corner.

Stella and all the guys are standing on the front steps, and Beau's there too. Oh my gosh, Beau is here! Except, something is obviously wrong. His lip is bleeding and Felix and Garrison look murderous.

"Stella?" Felix's gaze is hard as he stares between Beau and Stella. "What the hell is going on?"

"Beau is the guy I've been talking to. We met at the airport. Neither of us knew the connection at first."

I look to Teddy.

His expression is hard, but he still speaks softly when he says, "That's Beau Ricci. He plays football for Colorado."

Garrison circles Stella and Beau, looking like a wild animal about to attack. "I have been dying to run into you off the field, Ricci." His voice carries in the quiet night. "Let's do this. Me and you."

"I didn't come here for a fight," Beau says.

"Too bad."

Garrison moves to punch him. Beau steps away from Stella, shielding her as much as possible.

Teddy's steps get quicker, and the two of us hurry over to the action.

Beau doesn't try to fight back, but he holds Garrison at arm's length, so he can't continue to hit him.

"Fight me, you piece of shit." Garrison lowers his head and lunges for him.

"No!" Stella yells. She steps forward like she's going to get between them.

Felix gets there first and places a hand on Garrison's chest. "Take a walk before someone else gets hurt."

"He broke my fucking foot." Garrison's voice rises. "My football career might be over because of this prick."

"You almost hit Stella. Take a fucking walk," Felix says again. "I need to talk to my sister."

Garrison looks annoyed at being ordered around by my brother, but finally relents. His shoulders fall and his fingers unfurl. "What the fuck ever, Walters." Garrison knocks into his shoulder as he blows past him.

I move to stand next to my sister. Tears stream down her face and she looks so defeated, it hurts my insides. She wraps her arms around my shoulders, clinging to me. Felix looks like he might murder someone. I glance around at everyone. My head spins. "I don't understand. What's going on?"

Felix's voice is hard and strained, like he's fighting to keep control. "We're just trying to figure out the same thing. Stella, please help me understand. Did you invite him here? Are you dating this asshole? Beau fucking Ricci, really?"

"She didn't invite me. I drove up to surprise her. She had nothing to do with this." Beau gives my sister a look that under normal circumstances would make my stomach flip, but right now, it's twisted in knots.

"I was going to tell you," Stella says, stepping back to Beau's side. "This isn't how I wanted you to find out, but yeah, we like each other."

Beau wraps an arm around her. Felix fumes at the action, and his jaw flexes.

"No." My brother slices a hand through the air, then runs it over his head. "This isn't happening. Stella, you can't date this guy. You know what he did to Garrison. His dirty hit cost him the season."

"That was an accident." Stella is steadfast in her loyalty. Always has been and for some reason, she's decided that Beau is worth it. I don't know what to think.

"I'd never take a guy out on purpose," Beau says. He has dark hair, full lips, and a square jaw—Stella is a sucker for a square jaw.

"Yeah-fucking-right." Garrison has circled back. He looks only slightly less pissed off. He steps toward Beau. When Felix tries to intervene again, he holds up a hand. "I'm cool."

He doesn't seem cool. His shirt is untucked and the balled fist at his side is red and swollen, but Felix lets him by. "You expect me to believe that shit, Ricci? You fucking coward."

"You don't even know me," Beau says with a small shrug. He wipes blood from his lip. Garrison gets in his face, but Beau doesn't back down. "I don't want to fight you, but I'm not walking away from Stella unless she tells me to."

Beau is different than I expected. All of Felix's teammates are ready to pounce, and he's so chill about it. Maybe because he's way outnumbered. Maybe he really does care for my sister enough that he's willing to get his face pounded.

"Okay, that's enough." Teddy's voice is low and controlled, and everyone listens. He glances at the entrance, where security guards are surveying the situation. "We need to take this somewhere else before they call the cops."

Felix nods. "Agreed. We're done here. It's time for you to leave, Ricci. Keep your dirty games to the field and leave my sister out of it."

Felix turns for his car. The rest of the guys are already piling in. We brought two vehicles tonight, but Stella and I rode with Felix. My brother tosses Teddy the keys to his Corvette. "Come on, Stell."

She doesn't budge from Beau's side.

"Stella," Felix says again.

"No," she says. "This is dumb. You can't tell me who to date.

Beau is a great guy. If you'd just take a breath and get to know him, you—"

"It's okay," Beau interrupts her when it's clear that Felix isn't listening. His voice lowers where only she and I can hear him. "Go with your brother. We'll talk tomorrow."

"I'm sorry. This wasn't supposed to go this way." A tear slides down her face.

He wipes it away with the pad of his thumb. "It's okay. Go, baby."

Chapter Fifteen

"YOU DIDN'T EVEN GIVE HIM A CHANCE!" Angry tears fill Stella's eyes. She leans forward from the back seat to yell at Felix.

Teddy is silent as he drives us back to the cabin. I hate when Stella and Felix fight. I'd usually be the one trying to make peace, but this is messy, and I don't know who is right here.

"You're catching me a little off guard here, Stell." Felix's voice is softer but still has an edge. "You and Beau Ricci?!"

"Yes!" She throws her hands up in the air. "He isn't the guy you think he is. He's funny witty, and sweet."

"Sweet?" Felix's voice rises in question. "He has a reputation for being a player."

"He likes to have a good time."

"The guy is a wrecking ball, Stell."

"I know, I know. You think he took Garrison out on purpose. I don't believe that for a second. You don't know him like I do."

At the cabin, we pile out of the car. Garrison is loud as he paces the front porch, obviously still riled up.

"Ah, shit," Teddy says. "I got him."

Felix lets out a long breath, then looks to Stella. "Let's talk about it tomorrow."

"There is nothing to talk about. I like him. I'm going to keep seeing him."

"How do you know he isn't just using you to piss me and the guys off?"

"That's a low blow even for you." She stalks off.

"Fuck," Felix mutters. He looks to me for backup, but I don't have any idea what to say.

I chase after Stella. I find her in the bedroom, packing.

"What are you doing?"

"I want to go home."

"Stell." I sit on the edge of the bed. "You caught everyone by surprise. Give him the night to calm down."

"No. I can't stay here and listen to them talk about what a shitty guy he is." She waves a hand toward the living room. She's not wrong. They are talking smack about Beau. "He is a good guy."

"I believe you," I say.

"You do?"

"Yeah." I inch closer. "I wish you would have told me."

"I wanted to. I almost did a hundred times. But I didn't want you to have to keep something from Felix. It was hard enough for me."

"What are you going to do?"

"I have no idea. But tonight, I want to curl up with Whiskers and sleep in my old bed."

"Are you sure? We can stay in here, watch a movie in bed or get really drunk."

"I'm sure. I want to go home and wake up tomorrow and forget this entire trip happened. Please?" she pleads and then sighs. "Oh crap. I'm sorry. You want to stay for Teddy."

"No. I mean, yes, but it's okay."

"Holl—" Her brown eyes are filled with so much pain, it makes my chest ache.

"If you want to go home, then let's go home. Whatever you need." I squeeze her hand for reassurance. "Let's go home."

It takes no time to pack up. Felix tries to talk us out of going back tonight, but he's still so pissed, he isn't very convincing. They both need time to cool off.

Our goodbyes are stiff, the entire mood of the cabin so different than it's been all week.

Teddy comes outside as I'm putting our stuff in the back. His shirt is untucked and the top two buttons are undone. His hands are shoved in his front pockets. "Is she okay?"

I shut the back and lean against it. "She's pissed. I can't blame her."

"Yeah." His jaw flexes.

I cross my arms at my stomach. "I can't believe Garrison."

Teddy's head tilts. "What do you mean?"

"He *punched* him. Without even hearing what he had to say. It just made everything worse. Now Felix and Stella are pissed at each other. It's a mess."

"He was looking out for Stella."

"Is that what he was doing? It seemed like he was just getting payback for his own shit."

One of Teddy's shoulders lifts in a shrug. "Maybe so, but can you really blame him? Ricci cost him his season and maybe next year's."

"You said yourself that the hit was clean."

"I said it was a tough call, but if I were Garrison, I'd have wanted to do the same thing. And he knew dating Stella was going to piss us off. Coming here was ballsy."

"How can you say that? You don't even know him."

He doesn't quite meet my eye as he says, "Drive safe. Get some rest."

Something about this whole scene, him not answering my

question, his words and almost dismissive tone, make my hackles come up. "You sound like my brother."

Instead of my boyfriend. But I don't say that part because we haven't really established that.

He rubs at the back of his neck. "I don't know what you want me to say."

Something? Anything?

I let out a breath as I compose my thoughts. For years, I've felt like Teddy only saw me as Felix's little sister, but he's never made me feel as small as I do right now. And worse, his words have left me questioning if I'm justified in my irritation. I don't know if he's right or if I am, but I want to talk about it.

This is not the goodbye I had in mind. I pictured kisses and promises to talk over the break, maybe making plans for when we get back to Valley, but Teddy and I stand awkwardly in front of each other, not knowing what to say.

"I should go," I say finally.

He nods curtly. "Yeah. Drive safe."

"You already said that," I mumble, and then I get in the Jeep and drive away from my winter wonderland.

Chapter Sixteen

"**M**OM AND DAD'S PLANE JUST LANDED," I say as I step into the living room. Stella is curled up on the couch with Whiskers.

She sits up and he jumps off and trots away, probably to go lie in the kitchen window—his favorite spot.

"Time to put on a happy face and fake some holiday cheer."

I laugh lightly. "Dad was already asking if we pulled out all the lights for the house. He's ready to go full Griswold."

Stella smiles, but it's so half-hearted that it makes my insides hurt. She hasn't wanted to talk about it at all. We both crashed as soon as we got back last night, and this morning, we watched Hallmark movies and ate junk food. She's still attached to her phone, but I haven't seen her texting as much.

Her willpower is far greater than mine. I haven't heard from Teddy, and it's killing me. We left things in such a weird place. I don't know how to move forward.

"Go take a shower. I'll pull out the lights and help Dad. Mom will want to unpack and start the laundry before she does anything else. Should buy you an hour or two."

"Thanks, Holly." She stands and picks up the discarded ice cream container and chip bag. "Is Teddy coming with Felix?"

"No. He's going to Lucas's house for break."

"Really?"

"He'd already made plans to go there. Plus, we didn't leave things in the best place."

"Why not?"

"I don't know. It just felt weird as we were leaving. I know he's Felix's best friend, but last night, he made me feel like when we were twelve and Felix's friends would come over and ignore us."

"I'm sorry my drama caused trouble for you."

"Teddy's actions are not on you."

She nods. "It was a crazy night. Maybe he'll change his mind and come here again."

"Maybe."

"Have you texted him to ask?"

"No," I admit.

"You want him to make the move this time?" One side of her mouth pulls up into a small smile.

"Is that wrong?"

"No. I get that. You deserve to have someone make the move."

The sound of the garage door opening cause both of us to freeze. I glance out the front window in time to see Felix's orange car pulling up.

I move into the kitchen to greet him as he comes inside through the mudroom. I wait, heart rate picking up speed, for another person to step in behind him, but the door swings closed.

"Hey," Felix says when he sees me. He drops his bag to the floor and his mouth pulls into a tight smile.

Slowly, Stella gets up and comes to join us. They stare at each other. I can almost see a giant cartoon bubble above my sister's head, waiting for Felix to apologize or say something. He doesn't.

She sighs, loudly. "I'm going to shower."

When she's gone, Felix says, "You pissed at me too?"

I think for a second. "No, but you two should talk."

"Yeah." He comes over and hugs me. I want to ask him about Teddy, but Mom and Dad pull up before I can get the words out.

With Stella in the shower, Felix and I are held captive to stories from their vacation.

They're tan and smiling. I can't remember the last time my mother didn't rush off to unpack, but she leans against the kitchen island and stares at Dad with this big cheesy grin.

Eventually, though, Dad's impatience and excitement break up story time and Felix and I are dragged outside to the storage shed. Dad rummages for everything he needs, handing off items and instructions for where to put the lights. He has a whole system that is not to be messed with.

"You and Teddy, huh?"

I blush. "Yeah. I mean, maybe. I'm not really sure where we left things."

Felix nods slowly.

"Is it weird?"

He thinks for a couple of seconds. "Not really. A little, maybe, but I can see it. Teddy is the best guy I know."

"Who knows if anything will happen when we get back to school," I say. I wait for him to offer up some form of reassurance. Usually I'd get that from Stella, but I haven't wanted to pile on to her Beau drama.

Felix gives a half-hearted shrug that is the furthest thing from reassuring.

Later, when all the lights are up, I leave Dad and Felix to admire our handiwork and wander back inside. Mom and Stella are in the living room, putting up an artificial tree.

My heart sinks. "I miss having a real tree."

"A real tree doesn't make sense this year. And the lots are probably picked over at this point."

Stella holds out the star for the top. "Want to do the honors?"

I brush off my disappointment and step forward. "Absolutely."

Mom gets takeout for dinner and then she and Dad head off to bed early, exhausted from their trip. Felix, Stella, and I move into the living room. The tree is lit up and I put on *Christmas Vacation*. It's awkward, since they're barely speaking, but at least they're not completely ignoring each other.

My brother's phone buzzes, and he pulls it from his pocket and then stands. "I think I'm going to head up to bed, too."

"Already?" I whine.

"I'm beat." He starts up the stairs, already tapping away on his phone.

"Did I miss something?" Stella asks. "Did he meet someone or is he just avoiding me?"

"Not that I know about, but you know Felix, he always has girls blowing up his phone."

We watch the movie for a few minutes in silence.

"Anything from Teddy?"

"No." I flip my phone over in my hand to stare at the blank screen.

"I'm sorry," she says.

"It's fine." I smile and go back to watching Chevy Chase.

"I know you're bummed and trying not to act like it, but it's okay to be sad or disappointed or whatever you feel." She takes my hand. "If Theodore doesn't see how completely amazing you are, then he's an idiot."

"Thanks, Stell."

"Beau has some cute friends."

I laugh. "Let's not give Felix a heart attack."

Chapter Seventeen

I'M THE FIRST TO WAKE UP ON CHRISTMAS MORNING. I know this because if Stella had woken first, she would already be in my room, jumping up and down with excitement. And Felix always sleeps in.

I don't know how he does it. I can't sleep in, no matter how late I stay up the night before. There is just something enchanting about Christmas morning. The air feels different, joyous, light, and yes, magical.

Throwing off the covers, I slide my feet into my reindeer slippers and shuffle out of my room. Mom and Dad's voices carry faintly from downstairs. I spend a few minutes in the bathroom, getting ready, and when I come out, Stella is up.

"Merry Christmas!"

She rubs sleep from her eyes and murmurs back, "Merry Christmas."

I wait for her, and we go downstairs together. To my absolute surprise, Felix is already up, dressed, and has a cup of coffee in his hands.

"Merry Christmas," he says, and tips his mug in greeting.

"Breakfast before or after presents?" Mom asks, setting out the flour for her traditional Christmas morning homemade biscuits. Every year she asks and every year, the answer is the same.

"Presents!" Dad shakes his head and smiles as he takes a step toward the living room. "Who could possibly eat before seeing what Santa brought?"

Felix, Stella, and I share amused glances before we follow him. Mom is always last, making us wait just a few minutes longer to get started. I think she does it to build the anticipation or maybe just to annoy Dad.

Stella gets to open the first present. When we were little, she somehow convinced Felix and me that because she's the youngest (by one minute!) she deserved to be first at something. I think she used that line to get her way a lot when we were younger, but this is the only thing that stuck.

She holds up a pair of swim goggles and smiles at Dad. "Thank you."

He winks. "Welcome."

After that, we tear into presents at random. I get some new books that were on my wish list, a bracelet, and new notebooks and pens.

Felix gets practice gear and clothes, and stuff for his apartment. He chuckles when he opens the present Stella and I got him. I wrapped it in a football poster I got from the Valley U bookstore and made sure his face was most prominent. He still hasn't gotten used to all the attention, which makes it slightly more tolerable that he's such a big deal.

"Thanks, guys," he says, eyes twinkling with laughter, as he holds up the 'World's Okayest Brother' mug.

All three of us get things we didn't ask for but always receive: new toothbrushes, floss sticks, vitamins, socks, and gift cards to Target and various fast-food restaurants.

By the time we're done, our gifts are stacked up in piles beside us and wrapping paper is strewn everywhere. Dad pulls on the new 'I survived the Griswold Family Christmas' sweatshirt we got him and begins to clean up. Mom heads straight for the kitchen to get breakfast going.

Felix says he's going to help Dad, which probably means he's going to nap, and Stella and I put on *A Christmas Story* and flit between watching our favorite scenes to helping Mom in the kitchen.

The day passes with all our usual tradition and merriment. As we gather around the dining room table for our Walters' Family Annual Christmas Day Ultimate Game-a-thon (for the record, I am not the one that came up with that awful title), Felix puts on his jacket and says he's going to meet up with some friends.

"On Christmas?" Mom asks.

"He knows he's no match for my mad skills," Dad says as he places his tiles on the board to kick off our Scrabble game.

Felix swings his keys around one finger. "I won't be long, promise. I'll be back in time for Boggle."

Stella sinks down in her chair beside me. Things are still tense between her and Felix. If they've talked it out, they haven't come to a resolution.

Stella says she still believes he's a good guy, but she can't deny that Felix got in her head a little, so she's letting things simmer. As I look closer, her phone is mysteriously not in sight. In fact, I don't think I've seen her texting all day. That would make two of us. After checking every hour, on the hour, for a text from Teddy, I gave up around dinner time and left my phone upstairs, so I couldn't torture myself with it.

Maybe everything is fine and he's just busy with Lucas and his family. Maybe what we had at the cabin was a moment, and nothing else will come of it. It's the not knowing that is the hardest.

"Ugh, you're killing us," Dad groans as I get a triple-word score. My second of the game and I'm officially out of letters.

"She cheats," Stella teases. "I swear she cheats somehow."

"I need more coffee." Mom covers a yawn as she stands. "I think I have jet lag."

Headlights flash in the front window.

"Back just in time," Dad says as he starts to put away Scrabble, and Stella gets Boggle from the game cabinet. "And it looks like he brought a friend."

My head snaps up. Sure enough, a second set of headlights turn into the driveway. My heart beats wildly, hope rising with it. I push out of my chair and heads to the front door.

Teddy's truck comes to a stop behind Felix's car. My feet have a mind of their own, moving quickly toward him. My brother grins as I round the front of Teddy's truck.

The driver's side door finally opens, and Teddy hops out with a hesitant smile. "Hey."

"Hi." I'm frozen three feet away from him. "What are you doing here?"

Felix shuffles toward the house, giving us some privacy.

"I wanted to call, but I wasn't sure what to say. I'm sorry about how we left things."

"Me too."

He steps closer and takes my hand.

I've missed him. After two years of dreaming of being with him, the reality was so much better.

"I want to be with you. Do you want to be with me, or did you just take looking out for your best friend's sister a little too far?" I add in a little laugh at the end, like I'm half-joking, but my pulse races while I wait for his answer.

"Felix is like a brother to me. He's my best friend. I owe him a lot. Of course, I'm always going to want to look out for you and Stella because of that."

"But?"

"I like you. I'd like you even if you weren't his sister. And it'd be a hell of a lot less complicated." He smiles tentatively. "I want to be with you too."

"We could have had this conversation over the phone, you know?"

Quiet laughter slips from his lips. "What can I say? I like how the Walters family does Christmas. And I also needed to deliver your present."

My parents and Stella file out of the house.

"'Theo!" Mom calls from the front porch. She is the only one that calls him that, but he doesn't seem to mind. "I'm so glad you could join us."

"Sorry to impose on your Christmas game night."

"It's no imposition," my dad says. "Come in, come in. Holly was just destroying us at Scrabble."

Teddy's lips twitch with amusement as he looks to me. "One second. I need to grab something out of my truck. Felix?"

My brother nods and he and Teddy go to the back of the truck. Felix lowers the tailgate and then the two of them pull out a tree. I gasp and move closer. A Grand fir.

"I heard you might need one of these," Teddy says, a slight flush painting his cheeks.

I toss my arms around him, breathing in him and the tree. His hands are occupied, trying not to drop the tree, but he leans into my touch and his lips brush against my temple. Felix chuckles. "I think she likes it."

Chapter Eighteen

THE NEXT TWO DAYS ARE PACKED FULL OF ALL THE holiday things we missed out on before Christmas. We bake cookies and other desserts with Mom, we make our gingerbread houses, we drive around and look at all the holiday lights in the neighborhoods that go all-out every year, and play games and watch movies. My heart is so happy.

Felix and Teddy leave tomorrow. The Valley U football team's season is over, but the guys are attending bowl games with some of their teammates and coaches. I swear they've been done for only a few weeks and they're both talking about off-season practices, summer camps, and going all the way next year.

Stella and I are planning to spend a few more days at home and then we'll all meet up at Valley. Felix and his roommates are having a New Year's Eve party at their apartment. I can't wait to spend more time with the guy lying next to me.

We're taking up one couch. My head rests on his chest and one of his big, beefy arms is slung around my waist. Felix is in the recliner, and Stella is sitting on the love seat. Teddy's chest rumbles with laughter at the movie. I glance up at him, the goofy smile on his face and the way the lights dance across his face and darken the shadows of his dimples through the light scruff that's appeared since he got here.

He catches me staring at him instead of the movie and dips his head to kiss me. "You're not watching the movie."

"Now neither are you," I quip back.

His laughter spills into my mouth. Soft kisses turn a little hungrier, and then something soft collides with the side of my head.

I pull back in time to see the pillow land on the floor next to the couch.

Felix holds another up like he's ready to launch it. "I'm cool with my best friend making out with my little sister, but you know, not in front of me."

Teddy runs a hand down the back of my head, tangling his fingers in my hair. "Noted, bro."

I look at him with outrage. "Just like that? He says stop and no more kissing?"

"Later." He winks.

"You're missing the best scene," Stella says. She turns the volume up as Kevin runs through the snowy park to give the pigeon lady a turtle dove.

She cries every single time.

After the movie is over, Felix gets to his feet. "I'm going to bed."

"Same." Stella pushes the throw blanket off her.

"Eight tomorrow morning?" Felix asks Teddy.

"I'll be ready."

"Night, Holl," Stella says. "See ya later, Theodore."

They go upstairs and it's just the two of us hanging out in the living room. Mom and Dad went to bed hours ago.

Last night was the same, we stayed up for hours talking and kissing. I didn't make it to my own bed until well after three in the morning.

I get up and go grab the present I wrapped and placed under the tree earlier today. I bring it back to the couch and sit it in front of him. "I have something for you."

"You didn't need to do that," he says, but smiles.

He tears into the paper with the biggest grin.

"It's just something silly," I say when he has the tin completely unwrapped.

He gives it a little shake and his brows rise in question. He pries the top off, and when he looks inside, his mouth falls open in surprise. "No way. You made gingersnaps!"

"Well, I tried."

He picks one up and takes a bite.

"Are they anything like what your mom used to make? I tried one before I iced them, but I wasn't sure."

He nods as he chews. "Exactly. You even got the icing right. One half-dipped in icing, the other plain."

Before he's even finished the one in his mouth, he picks up another. "I forgot how good these are."

"Let me taste." I reach for one, but Teddy moves the tin, holding it up where I can't get any, and takes another bite.

"Hey!" I exclaim playfully.

He keeps the tin up high as he makes a big show of throwing his head back and closing his eyes as he chews. A sexy groan escapes. He mumbles around the cookie, "So good."

Instead of making another attempt at reaching the cookies, I crawl into his lap. I wrap my legs around him and press our chests together.

"You don't share very well."

"They were a gift," he says when he's done chewing, "from my girlfriend."

My brows lift.

"I mean, if that's what she wants to be."

"She wants to be."

His mouth descends on mine. He tastes like ginger and sugar. We kiss until my body trembles and we're both panting, then we move to the floor in front of the Christmas tree. Mom was so tickled that Teddy brought us a tree, she moved the artificial one we had in the living room to the dining room, and put his in its spot. I love how it smells and the way it looks, but mostly, I love how he knew the perfect thing to get me. He was paying attention that day at the tree lot. Maybe he always was.

As he lavishes me with long, sweet kisses, he pulls my shirt over my head. The way he looks at me, my desire mirrored back, makes my body flush.

His hand slides around the back of my neck and draws me closer. "You're so beautiful, Holly."

He fingers the necklace, running his thumb over my name.

We fall to the ground. Our kisses are more urgent as we strip each other down.

I climb on top of him. His dick nudges my entrance, and he shifts, so he isn't poking me. "I don't have a condom." His hands roam over my side, back, and up to cup my breasts. "Think your brother is asleep yet?"

"You are so not asking my brother for a condom."

He scrunches up his nose. "Yeah, that'd be weird."

I lean over him, my boobs are conveniently in his face, and he takes advantage of the position to capture one in his mouth. Reaching under the tree skirt, I pull out the strip of condoms I put there with the cookies.

I sit back and hold them up, letting them dangle from my fingers.

His chest moves in a quiet laugh. "Under the tree?"

"I couldn't think where else to stash them."

"What if someone else had found them?"

I lift one shoulder and let it fall. "I would have blamed Felix."

Laughing, he pulls me back down to him and then rolls us, so he's on top.

"Are you sure?" he asks, staring down at me with those soft gray eyes.

"Positive." I beam up at him. "I've dreamt about this for so long."

He dips his head to place a kiss above my belly button.

While his mouth travels lower, his gaze flicks up to mine. "Me too, sweetheart."

He leaves a trail of wet kisses down my stomach and on my inner thigh. His broad shoulders push my legs apart. He hooks an arm around one, opening me wider to him, and his mouth covers my sensitive core. His tongue flattens and then flicks across the bundle of nerves.

My body is liquid heat as he brings me closer and closer to the edge. Only when I'm panting and muttering his name on an endless loop does Teddy roll on a condom and position himself.

He slides in slowly, disappearing inside me an inch at a time. He stills when he's fully buried. I hold my breath and dig my fingernails into his forearms. It's so good. Too good. And the man hasn't even moved.

He drives in gently at first, but we're both too close and too amped up. We won't last long, no matter how slow and sweet he goes.

I come with his name on my lips, and he follows a second later, swallowing my words and kissing me like he'll never get enough.

He falls to the floor beside me, immediately finding my hand and lacing our fingers together.

"That was . . ." I trail off as I gulp in air.

"Yeah," he rasps.

I let my head fall to the side, so I can stare at him. His happy, satiated smile re-energizes me.

"Again?"

He barks a laugh. "Yeah, sweetheart. Again."

"A million times more?"

"A million and one." He drags the pad of his thumb along my lower lip, leans closer, and then gives me a soft kiss.

"A million and two?"

His smile widens.

"A million and three?"

"Mhmm." He chuckles. "But first, I need another gingersnap."

"Are you finally going to share?"

We sit up, and Teddy grabs the tin of cookies. While he's distracted by my bare chest, I steal the tin from him. His arms wrap around me a second later. He whispers petty threats for all of two seconds before his mouth finds my neck.

I finally get a bite of his precious gingersnaps. And he gets me. Again.

And again.

Epilogue

Teddy

A HOT GIRL STANDS IN THE OPEN DOORWAY OF MY bedroom. Music from the party is loud, and the bass vibrates the floor.

The girl pops a hip and gives me a sweet, sultry smile. Her red hair is down in loose curls around her shoulders. She fingers one strand as she smiles shyly. Sexy black boots cover her legs all the way up to her thighs.

Everyone dressed up tonight, including her. The black dress hugs her frame in all the right places. "Hi, Teddy."

She's a very hot girl, but she's not *my* hot girl.

"Hey, Stella."

She lets her hand drop to her side and smiles. "How do you always know? Even Felix did a double-take with my hair all down and done up like Holly's."

"You look nice," I tell her, then *my* girl steps around her into the room.

She has on a gold dress and a pair of matching strappy shoes that lace up her toned legs. Her hair is down, and she has on a Happy New Year headband. She wouldn't be my girl without a little extra holiday cheer.

The truth is, I don't need to be able to tell them apart (though I can). It's a feeling when Holly is nearby. From the moment I met her, I knew she was someone I wanted to get to know better. At first, it was because she was my best friend's sister. Felix and I clicked right off the bat. Within days, he felt like family. So naturally, when his parents and sisters came to visit, I wanted to meet the people he talked about so much.

The Walters family is tight. Something my family used to be. I miss that.

But with every interaction with Holly, I was more intrigued. I like how she's slow to speak, but eager to listen. She makes people feel seen and heard and important. She doesn't offer up a lot of herself, but it just makes people all the more curious.

I like how she knows every word to the movie *Elf*, and when she laughs, her entire body shakes with the movement.

It's a hundred different things, and counting, that I like about Holly. I can't wait to discover more.

As discreetly as possible, I grab the gift box from my desk drawer and shove it in my pocket. She crosses the small room in the house I share with Felix and Lucas, and I meet her halfway and wrap an arm around her waist. "Hey, sweetheart."

She loves it when I call her that. Her cheeks flush and the flecks of green in her eyes are more prominent.

"Hi." Her voice is breathy as she leans into me.

"Okay, well. I'm out of here," Stella says. As she leaves, she calls, "You passed the test, Theodore."

Laughing, Holly faces me and presses her body flush against mine. "I have something for you."

"Oh yeah." I run my hands along her back and dip my head down to kiss her.

"It's in the kitchen."

"So far away." I press her tighter against me and kiss her again. Now that we're both back at Valley, we've been spending days and nights together. I figure we have at least a year or two of making up for lost time.

"Come on," she says, taking my hand and pulling me out to the party.

There are a lot of people crammed into our place. It's an old three-bedroom house, two blocks from campus. The keg is out back on the patio and liquor bottles are lined up on the kitchen counter. The door to the backyard is propped open, and people filter in and out.

Holly walks into the kitchen and then turns around. She drops her hand to the counter. "I left it right here."

"You left what here?" I ask, pouring myself a drink.

"A headband that matches mine. I thought tonight, you and I could be twins."

I scan the counter and then beyond to the living room. My lips pull up into a smile when I spot Lucas.

"Found it," I say and point to him. He has on the headband with a neon pink T-shirt that says, 'Happy New Year,' in messy Sharpie handwriting, and also about a dozen beaded necklaces. He is next-level festive and dancing in a group of girls.

"Lucas!" she yells, but he doesn't hear her over the music.

"It's all right. I swiped these from someone earlier." I pull a pair of paper glasses with the new year in big font across the top and slide them on my face.

The smile she gives me makes the uncomfortable and silly thing worth it.

"Now let's dance, sweetheart."

We join the dozens of others crammed into the living room, dancing until we're both exhausted. The night, and the year, is ticking by. The countdown is on. Five minutes left in the best year of my life.

Holly and I get drinks and then go outside to get some fresh air. She snuggles close to me to keep warm.

I slide the glasses onto the top of my head. "I have something for you."

Her brows lift in intrigue. "Sparklers?"

"No." I chuckle. "But that would have been a good idea."

I pull the box from my pocket and hold it out to her.

She takes it hesitantly. "Teddy. You didn't need to get me anything."

"I know. And I didn't. At least not how you think. It was my mother's."

Her brown eyes grow larger, and she tries to hand it back. "Teddy. I can't—"

I push it back toward her. "You can. Open it."

Holly flips open the jewelry box and peers inside. Her head tilts to the side as she smiles and then brings a finger to run over the green holly leaves.

"I told you, she liked the holidays too. She had a bunch of holiday jewelry. I kept thinking about this necklace while we were at the cabin. I couldn't remember for sure if it was holly leaves or if I'd just convinced myself that because I wanted to make some cosmic connection between you two. I asked my dad to look around and see if he could find it."

After I told him about Holly, he was happy to track it down and send it. We don't have the same type of relationship as the Walters family, but we're working on it. I told my dad and brother I was coming home for Christmas next year, no matter what. It'll never be the same without Mom, but it doesn't mean the three of us can't be together and find our own way to keep celebrating.

"It's beautiful, Teddy. Will you help me put it on?" She takes it from the box and holds it around her neck for me to clasp. Once it's on, she touches the necklace and smiles. "Thank you."

"You're welcome. She would have loved you." I swallow around the lump in my throat. "Because I love you, Holly. I know we've only been dating a short while, but I've been falling for you a little at a time for as long as I've known you."

Her lips part, but she doesn't speak.

"I'm sorry. Shit, did I freak you out?"

Her head slowly shakes side to side. "No. I love you too."

People begin to countdown. "Ten. Nine. Eight."

I don't wait for one, I kiss her. We're still making up for lost time, after all, and I don't want to waste a single second.

Sneaking Around with the Player

Chapter One

Beau

"Yo, Ricci." Aaron juts his chin in acknowledgment as we get to the gate for our flight. "A bunch of the guys are going to grab dinner. You in?"

I drop my backpack onto a seat by the window looking out at the runway and take the chair next to it. "Nah, I'm good."

"Shake it off. We'll get them next time."

"Yeah." Nodding, I give my buddy a playful smile that is all show. "Of course, we will."

When my teammates are finally gone, I let out a breath and put on my headphones. I don't feel like listening to music, but it helps drown out some of the airport noise.

We are catching a flight back to Colorado after a tough loss. All losses are tough, but this one stings especially bad for me because I should have stopped the final play, the one that let the other team take a one-point lead with three seconds left.

I'm a cornerback. THE cornerback. The best on my team, maybe in the entire conference. I'm known for my ability to anticipate plays, my quick reflexes, and my all-out, never-give-up mentality.

Once you get me started, there's no stopping me. Some call me reckless or destructive. Some call me determined. I don't know which is right. I'm just trying to do my best for my team and for my family cheering me on from home. It means everything to them that I'm playing college ball.

I see a new text from my dad, ignore it, and pull up Twitch to watch my favorite gamer. This guy is legit. He's a world-class speedrunner on Super Mario. I wonder if his parents critique his every game. Probably not.

While I watch, the seats around me start to fill up. It's the weekend before Thanksgiving, so there are a lot of families, just a lot of people in general.

A shadow falls over me and I glance up to find a girl looking at me with big, brown eyes, like she might have said something I didn't hear.

"Sorry. Did you say something?" I ask as I move one headphone off my ear.

"Are you saving that for someone?" She points to the chair next to me, where my backpack sits.

"No. It's all yours." I move my bag to the floor in front of me and she drops into the chair.

"Thank you," she says with a sigh. "You just saved me from watching my ex and his new girlfriend make out like they're about to get on two different flights. Making out at the airport should be reserved for couples who are parting ways, or are reuniting, or I don't know, anyone but them."

I give her my attention, which prompts her to add, "That sounded mean, didn't it?"

"A little, maybe."

"Sorry. Ignore me." She waves a hand and slumps in the chair. Without looking at me, she says, "Thank you for the seat."

I do ignore her, for a moment. My hand goes to pull my headphone back over my ear, but then I stop. She's more interesting than anything I have on my phone to kill the time. "But it's also pretty insensitive to make out with someone in front of an ex that you know still likes you."

"Oh, I don't like him." She undoes the braid in her hair. It's a light red that could almost be confused as blonde, if the light from the window at our backs wasn't hitting it just right. She finger combs it, and then begins to braid it again. "You don't believe me?"

"I didn't say that."

"I could see it on your face," she says. She pulls her feet up into the chair, crossing her legs like the airport chair is roomy—it is not. "I broke up with him."

"Then why does it annoy you so much?"

She thinks for a second, which gives me a chance to check her out more closely. Her skin is fair, which makes her brown eyes and long, black lashes stand out. Her lips are shiny and pink, and as she thinks, she purses them slightly. The center of her top lip is wider than the bottom, making a perfect heart. She's wearing a Valley U Swim & Dive Team sweatshirt with black athletic pants and sneakers.

"I think relationships require a mourning period when they're over. A time to think about what went well, what went wrong, how that person was or wasn't the right fit."

"Yeah, I don't know any guy that does that. Sorry. We pretty much live by the get-drunk-and-move-on-to-forget philosophy."

She laughs, a soft sound that makes her lips pull apart to show off straight, white teeth. She has a great smile.

"Why'd you break up with him?" I find myself wanting to know more, to prolong this conversation. She's a perfect distraction.

"You're gonna think it's dumb."

"Well, now I definitely have to know."

She angles her body toward me. "He whistles."

My brows rise. "Whistles?"

"Yeah. Like all the freaking time. At first, I thought it was sort of endearing, but it's all the time. While he's watching TV, walking to class, in class, *during sex*."

"He whistles during sex?" I bark a laugh, then cover it with a fist.

She nods adamantly. "If he wasn't under the water or my

mouth wasn't plastered to his, then he's whistling. And don't get me wrong, I love kissing, but my lips were chapped, and I just couldn't take it anymore."

"Under the water?"

"He's a swimmer."

"Ah. Did you ask him about it?"

"He was like, 'Oh, yeah. I don't even realize I'm doing it.'" She grimaces. "And I realize it's a stupid reason to break up with someone, but I couldn't imagine myself getting used to it. Not with him. And I guess that's really the thing. If it's the right person, you shouldn't want to choke them for their annoying, quirky habits, right?"

"Probably not." I whistle, just to poke a little fun at her, but then laugh.

"See? It's not annoying when you do it. Not yet at least." She settles back into her chair.

"Not until we're dating for a month or two and you're looking for an excuse to break up with me?"

"You should be so lucky." There's a sassy glint in her eyes that makes my pulse kick up a notch.

"You're a swimmer, too?" I ask, pointing at her sweatshirt. "Or still wearing his clothes even though you claim to be over him?"

"I *am* over him, and I'm a diver."

"A diver. No shit? Like flipping in the air from a really high diving board?" I make a circular motion with my pointer finger.

Her mouth pulls into another big smile. "Yep. It's called a platform or a springboard."

"That's awesome. How'd you get into that?"

"I did swim team every summer when I was a kid, and then in middle school, I started diving." She shrugs.

"That's really cool." I move my headphones down around my neck. "You're coming from a game? Meet? Competition? I just realized I don't know what they call swimming events."

"Meets. And yes. We were at UT and now we're heading home."

"Did you win?"

"We did," she says proudly.

"Nice. Congrats."

"Thanks. Do you go to CU?" She points to my sweatshirt with the college name written across the front.

"Yeah."

"Are you heading home for Thanksgiving?"

"No, I—"

I'm cut off when she ducks low in her seat and mutters, "Oh, crap."

I look around us to figure out why she's freaking out, but everyone near us is minding their own business and perfectly calm. "Are you okay?"

"My ex," she whispers. "Two o'clock. Blue hat, standing a foot above everyone else. Cute blonde attached to his hip."

I find the guy. He is tall. Lean and lanky, making him seem even taller. I'm six foot one, and I doubt he's more than a few inches taller than me. The chick beside him stares up at him adoringly. She's wearing a sweatshirt, just like the girl next to me.

"Are they gone?" she asks, still hiding.

"No."

She sits up a little straighter and peers around me at the same moment he scans the crowd.

"What is he doing here?" She whisper-hisses and ducks back down, moving a little closer to me like she's using me as a shield. She smells nice, like mint and flowers. "Our gate is all the way at the other end of the terminal."

After a thorough glance around the gate (I'm half-convinced he's looking for the girl hiding next to me), he walks in the opposite direction, hand in hand with his new girlfriend.

"They're going," I say.

She lets out a breath and sits tall, but still close to me. She

113

has freckles across the bridge of her nose, and I've finally placed the minty smell—wintergreen gum. Her eyes lock on mine and we both freeze for a moment, before my phone captures her attention. "What are you watching?"

She moves away, but still stares down at the screen in my hand.

"Twitch."

"Speedrunning?" she asks, still staring down.

"Yeah. You know it?"

"Beating games superfast." She nods. "I've seen some of those. My brother was obsessed with it when we were younger. He used to drive me crazy when we'd play video games together because I'd be trying to get all the coins and check things out, and he was racing to the finish or finding glitches to skip levels."

"You have a brother?"

"And sister. You?"

"No. Only child. Lots of cousins, though."

"Can I creepily watch over your shoulder?"

"No need to creep," I say, and angle my phone so she can watch. I take my headphones from around my neck and hold them between us.

With a smile, she leans closer, resting her ear to one side, while I listen through the other. And that's how we kill the next twenty minutes.

It's . . . nice. We only talk to comment on the stream, but I'm having a good time and can't seem to stop stealing glances at her.

The lull of the airport noise around us just sort of fades away. After a game, I like to have space. I need time to get my head straight, digest the good and bad from the game, read through the texts my dad always sends with feedback (mostly criticism), and let it all drift away so I can go back to being the happy-go-lucky guy everyone expects. But right now, I'm not thinking about anything but the girl next to me.

When the attendant working the closest gate announces that

we're about to start boarding, we both snap out of our happy bubble.

"Looks like you're about to leave."

"Yeah," I say, and swivel until I locate my teammates. They're three rows over, a mass of red. "What time does your flight leave?"

She looks at her watch. "Oh crap. We started boarding fifteen minutes ago."

While she scrambles to get her stuff together, I stand and wait for her. Something like disappointment tugs at me.

"Do you want me to AirDrop you the link to the stream?" It's a weak attempt to prolong some sort of contact with her. She's hot and I had a good time.

"Yeah. That'd be great. I have a feeling I'm going to need a distraction on the flight home."

"Cool."

"Thanks. This was fun." She waves with a hand around the strap of her backpack and then starts to takes off for her gate.

I grab the link and am about to send it to her, when she pauses in her tracks. "Text it to me. I don't have AirDrop turned on for non-contacts." She rattles off her phone number.

I walk with her, since she really needs to get on her plane before it leaves, repeating her number back to her as I tap it into my phone.

"Got it."

She smiles a little more timidly than she has since she walked up and asked to sit beside me. "Thanks. I really better hurry. It was nice hanging with you."

"Yeah," I agree.

I keep following, walking away from my gate, as she puts space between us to get to her flight. She looks over her shoulder and finds me still looking at her, then hits me with another smile.

"I didn't even get your name," I yell. "I'm Beau."

"Stella." She jogs backward. "Stella Walters."

Chapter Two

Stella

> **Me:** *I made it back. Thanks for the link. It provided a nice distraction. Guess who sat across the aisle from me on the plane?*
>
> **Beau:** *Harry Styles?*
>
> **Me:** *No. Why would I want a distraction from Harry Styles??!!*
>
> **Beau:** *Good point. Must have been the whistling ex then. Hope everyone on the flight had ear plugs. I'm glad I could help.*

I STARE DOWN AT OUR TEXT EXCHANGE, RE-READING IT again and wondering if I should text back. He was nice. Cute, too. Dark hair, square jaw, athletic build with trendy gold, circle-rimmed glasses that gave him a whole hot, studious, muscled-nerd vibe.

I *think* he was into me. If I'm totally honest, it was hard to read him. But I assume the whole asking to send me the link thing was a ploy to get my number. Although his text doesn't leave a lot of room for a reply.

I got back to campus over an hour ago and came straight to

my dorm to shower and get ready for a night out. My brother Felix is having a party at his place. He shares a house off-campus with two other football players.

I should already be there, but I've been wracking my brain for something clever to text Beau. Shoving my phone into my purse, I head out. Holly will know what to say. She's better with the written word.

At Felix's house, I knock on the front door, but go in without waiting for an answer. Even if they could hear me over the music playing inside, they'd just yell, "Door's open," or "Come in." Getting up and answering the door for guests is entirely too formal for anything that happens inside.

"Hello?" I call as I walk into the living room. It's empty, but above the fireplace on the mantle, a speaker sits between empty beer bottles, blasting music.

The house has bedrooms on both sides of the living room. Felix's roommates, Teddy and Lucas, are on one side and Felix has the other with a small, private bathroom that he won in a drinking game.

I go straight back to the eat-in kitchen. It looks out onto a patio, where the guys have thrown many parties, like the one happening later tonight.

Sliding open the door, I step outside. The keg is tapped and sitting in a big, red plastic bin in the middle of the yard. Felix and several other guys are playing washers, but Holly is sitting at a table with some of the football guys' girlfriends and looks up immediately. I can read the 'thank god you're finally here' look on her face so well, a small laugh escapes my lips.

Holly and I are identical twins. We share the same strawberry blonde hair color and brown eyes. We even have the same number of freckles on our right arm—we counted once.

She gets up to greet me, wrapping an arm around my neck as she does. "I am so glad you're here. What took so long?"

"Sorry. I got distracted." I give her a playful smile, which she acknowledges immediately.

"Who is he?"

"Stella!" Felix calls from where he's playing washers. His roommate and best friend Teddy stands next to him and lifts his cup in a silent greeting.

"I'll tell you all about it later." I link my arm through hers. "Have you talked to Teddy tonight?"

Color stains her cheeks. "Yeah. He said hello and asked how classes were going."

My twin has had a crush on our brother's best friend for as long as we've known him. I think he might like her too, but they're both so freaking polite to each other, it's not likely either is ever going to pick up on it.

"Did he use your name?" I lower my voice and do my best impression of the quiet and broody football player. "Hey, Holly. How are your classes going? I could give you a little one-on-one tutoring if you want." I waggle my eyebrows.

"Oh my gosh. Stop it." She nudges me with an elbow. "He did not say that. He'd never."

"But he did use your name, didn't he?"

She nods slightly.

"He definitely likes you."

People get us mixed up all the time. It was better in high school because our friends had known us for years, but we've only been at Valley U for a few months, and we're constantly being called by the wrong names. But never Teddy. It's worth noting he never greets me by name.

As we get closer to the guys, Felix comes forward and hugs me with one arm. "You made it. How was the meet?"

"First place in both my dives."

He pulls back and lifts a fist for me to bump. "Congrats."

"Thanks."

Standing next to me, Holly has gone quiet and stiff. I glance over at the point of her unease. "Hey, Theodore."

One side of Teddy's lips quirks up. He has dimples, one of the many things Holly adores about him, and one pops out now. "Hey. Congrats on the meet."

"Thank you." I pull Holly a step closer. "How've you been?"

The guys go back to tossing washers while we talk, and then Holly and I jump in for the next game. I love watching Teddy and my sister sneak little glances at each other. Holly is generally more timid and shy than me, but Teddy is a popular football player so I haven't figured out why he hasn't made a move. Maybe because of Felix? Our brother is pretty protective of us, but Teddy is a great guy.

Two hours later, the party is really going. The backyard is filled with people, more are inside. Holly and I head into the kitchen and find Teddy and Lucas playing video games in the living room, which reminds me of Beau.

"Hey, Stella," Lucas yells from the couch, but he's looking at my sister. His gaze darts between us. "Ah shit. One of you, grab me a beer from the fridge?"

"One of us?" I arch a brow.

"I tried."

"Dude, there's a keg outside," Teddy says without looking away from the TV.

"I'm not drinking that crappy light shit," Lucas replies to him, while giving Holly and me a pouty face with sad, puppy eyes.

Chuckling, I do get him a beer, but then I toss it so it's good and shaken up. Maybe it'll spray all over him.

Pulling out my phone, I'm struck with a surprising amount of disappointment that I don't have any new texts from Beau. I really thought he was into me. Maybe I completely misread his kindness as something more. Or worse, maybe he was taking pity on me because I was yammering on about my ex. Ugh.

119

Holly pours us both a drink. "Okay. I've waited patiently, played three games of washers, flip cup—which you know I hate."

"It's so fun."

"And stressful. I can't concentrate with everyone watching me."

I laugh because it's such a Holly answer. Always happy to be out of the spotlight.

"Tell me who it is," she begs.

"Who?"

"The guy you're talking to. It isn't Eric again, is it?"

"No."

"Another guy on the swim team?"

I shake my head.

"Who?!" Her brown eyes plead with me.

"His name is Beau. I met him at the airport."

Her lips part as if she's going to speak, but it's several seconds before she says, "Only you would meet a guy at the airport. How did this happen? Does he go to Valley?"

I tell her the whole story. How I was trying to get away from Eric and how I gave Beau my number. She wants to see the texts, obviously, and I drum my nails against my thigh as I wait for her assessment.

"His texts are cute. Flirty and fun. I'd say he's into you."

"You got all that off a few texts, but you can't see how totally into you Teddy is from across the room?"

"Shhh." She thrusts my phone back at me. "Text him back now."

"And say what?"

"Anything."

"That's too broad."

"Okay." She puts a finger to her chin. "You need some common ground. You know that he goes to college and he likes video games. Anything else?"

"I know that he's very cute."

"If you respond by telling him how hot he is, he'll either think you're a potential stalker or that you're looking to sext." She casts a serious stare in my direction. "Are you just looking to sext?"

"No," I say defensively. "Sexting is so high school."

Holly laughs. I feel a prick of unease. I don't have the best track record when it comes to dating, but at least I put myself out there.

"But I get your point." I scrunch up my nose. "I already thanked him for the link. I don't know how to spin that into another conversation."

"Text him and ask for more video game stream suggestions."

"He'll see right through that."

"If he likes you, he won't care."

"And if he doesn't like me?"

"Who would dare not like you?" She bumps her shoulder against mine. "Worst case, he'll ignore you or he'll hit you up with a bunch of links and nothing else. At least then you'll know. No big loss, right?"

"Right." I let out a breath.

"You really like this guy."

"I just met him."

"So?" She casts a quick glance to where Teddy sits in the living room playing video games. "Sometimes it's just that fast."

Chapter Three

Beau

Stella: Any more streaming suggestions? I have another meet next weekend.

I'VE STARTED TO REPLY TO HER TEXT A DOZEN TIMES. IT's an innocent question, but I can't bring myself to answer.

"Still torturing yourself?" Aaron asks as he takes a seat in front of his locker, the one next to mine. We finished practice twenty minutes ago, but I've only made it as far as taking off my jersey and pads.

Stella Walters has consumed my thoughts for two days now. We spent less than an hour together, I know hardly anything about her, and yet, I can't remember the last time I enjoyed spending time with someone that much.

I lock the screen and tuck my phone into my backpack, then drop down onto the bench in front of me. "Nah. Just checking email."

"Bullshit." He pulls on a clean T-shirt and then runs his hands over the wet strands of his hair. "Text her back. Who cares that she's Felix Walter's little sister?"

I cut him with a look meant to silence him, but Aaron laughs. "Seriously. We don't play Valley U again this year. Who cares?"

If Walters is anything like I think he is, he'll care. A hell of a lot.

We've been playing against each other for years. I'm from Arizona, same as him. We played against each other the first time in middle school and met countless times in high school, but our real rivalry started senior year. We went head-to-head for the high school championship (he won), then we both went to Pac-12 colleges, and last year, when we played Valley he won again.

I finally got a victory against the talented quarterback this year, but it wasn't easy. It came on the back of a controversial call. I tackled one of their wide receivers as he was going out of bounds. Garrison Hamilton is known for slipping by the defense, finding holes, and cutting to the middle, just when it looks like he's going down.

Hamilton is good, but also a giant asshole. I've never met someone that talks more trash on the field than him. He knows how to get under your skin. I studied tape of him for weeks leading up to the game and I was ready. I wasn't letting him get in my head, and I wasn't letting him past me for a touchdown. Valley wanted a penalty for a late hit, but ultimately, it was ruled in our favor.

All of that would have been enough to piss off Walters and his team, but that's nothing new for college football. We have rivalries between schools for all sorts of reasons. It helps keep our edge, makes us dig a little harder for every game. But Garrison was injured on the play, which sent Valley into an uproar. If it hadn't been the final seconds of the game, I'm convinced there would have been a brawl on the field.

Listen, it happens. I never want to injure someone out there, but that's basically impossible. Two dudes flying at each other with the force of a Mack truck, someone is bound to get hurt. This time it was on their side, and they'll be out for blood the next time we meet.

So, no, I don't think Walters is going to be cool with me texting his sister.

I hoped it was coincidence. Walters is a common last name, right? She wasn't hard to find on social media and it confirmed what I knew in my gut the second she told me her name. Stella is my long-time football rival's little sister.

"Okay. I can see by that stubborn look on your face, that you aren't going to listen to me." Aaron stands. "Mind if I hit her up?"

I scowl at him.

"Kidding." He laughs. "Do you want to grab a beer?"

"I can't tonight. I have a test in the morning, and I need to pass or Coach is going to be on my ass about my grades again." Tomorrow is the last day of classes before Thanksgiving break. We get three days off school, but that just means more football. We play Baylor at home on Saturday, and those three days without classes will be spent on the field, preparing for the game.

"All right. Text me if you change your mind or need a study break."

He leaves, and after a quick shower, I get dressed and do the same. Aaron and I share a dorm room in Webber Hall. Since he's out for the night, I have the suite to myself. It's a decent-sized space. We have separate bedrooms and share a bathroom, kitchen, and small living room, where we have a TV and couch. We're planning on moving out of the dorms next year, but this isn't a bad setup. And it's close to the practice facilities.

I sit on the couch, laptop in front of me. I read over my biology notes and then the last three quizzes. I keep studying until my eyes start to glaze over and I'm confident I can at least eke out a passing grade on the test.

I might have partied a little too hard early in the semester. And all last year. And my entire high school career. My priorities have always been football, fun, then grades. But the latter has nearly cost me playing time. If I don't keep a certain GPA, I'm benched. So, I've had to adjust. I think I've finally found a balance between studying and everything else, but I won't be making the dean's list anytime soon.

I glance to my left, where my cell phone sits on the couch beside me.

Don't do it.

Even as I think the words, I grab my phone and pull up Stella's text. As I'm re-reading it for the hundredth time, three dots appear, indicating she's typing.

My pulse accelerates as I wait. The dots stop and then start again. I didn't expect her to text again. Stella doesn't seem like the kind of girl to chase after a guy, and my non-response shut down the friendly back and forth we had going.

I know I shouldn't want her to keep trying to talk to me, but the way adrenaline continues to rush through me while I grip the phone tightly in my hand, I have absolutely no chill. I'm losing my mind. The dots disappear again and don't start back up. Maybe they were faulty dots? Is that a thing?

Fuck it, I don't owe Walters anything. And it's just a little friendly texting, anyway.

Chapter Four

Stella

Beau: Check out this guy. And there's this girl I think you might like too. She's on now.

I'LL ADMIT, IT TOOK EVERYTHING IN ME NOT TO SEND A second text. I stand firmly in the belief that if a guy can't find five seconds to text back, he's just not that into you. However, Holly suggested I send one more text. A little nudge. She said, "If he doesn't reply within the hour, then delete his contact and move on."

In the end, I couldn't do it. But then Beau texted seconds later. What kind of crazy coincidence is that?

"Now what do I say?" I ask, panic and excitement coursing through me.

My sister sets her book down and comes over from her side of the room to sit on the bed in front of me. "Thank him and then ask him what he's up to."

Me: Thank you!

"You left off the other part. He doesn't have anything to respond back to." Holly's brows adorably scrunch together.

"Wait for it." I stare at the screen, hoping I'm not wrong.

Beau: How's your week going?

Holly's lips part and she stares at me in disbelief. "Clearly, you don't need me. You've got this. In fact, I need a little of your dating skills."

"We're not dating. I just met him."

"You're in the pre-dating stage."

"No. I don't think so."

"Then what's the point?"

"A little flirty texting. You should try it. You do have Teddy's number, don't you?"

Pink dots her cheeks.

"I bet Teddy would loooove some flirty texts. Want me to help you draft something?"

"Just stick to your own flirty texts."

"Suit yourself."

> *Me: Good. Yours? Plans for Thanksgiving break?*
>
> *Beau: Week's been good. Nothing exciting planned for break. What about you?*
>
> *Me: No meets this weekend, but I'm staying in Valley. My brother plays football, did I tell you that? He has a game and my parents are coming to watch.*

This time it takes him longer to respond.

> *Beau: You didn't tell me that. That's cool.*

And a second later, another.

> *Beau: Did you check out the link I sent you? That girl is pretty badass.*

Holly gets up and goes back to her own bed and picks up her abandoned paperback. It's not even Thanksgiving and my twin already has Christmas lights strung along the wall above her bed. I don't know anyone that loves the holidays more than her.

"You're smiling so big."

She's not wrong. I'm downright giddy. I love this stage of meeting a guy. All the fun, get-to-know-you back and forth. It's the weeks or months later when that excitement wears off that I find myself noticing all the red flags and annoying habits that I can't look past.

> *Me: Are you watching right now?*
>
> *Beau: Yep. And studying. Or I was studying.*
>
> *Me: Test tomorrow?*
>
> *Beau: Yeah.*
>
> *Me: What year are you?*
>
> *Beau: Sophomore. You?*
>
> *Me: Freshman.*

We didn't share a lot of personal information at the airport, so we get the basics out of the way. I learn that Beau is majoring in history, that he isn't exactly sure what he wants to do with said degree, and that he just celebrated his birthday in September.

> *Me: Are you dating anyone?*
>
> *Beau: No.*
>
> *Me: Why not?*
>
> *Beau: What do you mean, why not?*
>
> *Me: Don't make me say it.*
>
> *Beau: ?*
>
> *Me: You're an attractive guy. So either you aren't interested in dating or you're an asshole?*
>
> *Beau: You're sure those are the only possible reasons?*
>
> *Me: Pretty sure. So which is it?*

> Beau: *Neither. I just don't have a lot of time for dating right now.*
>
> Me: *That's weak.*
>
> Beau: *It's true. I have a lot going on.*
>
> Me: *Do you have a job?*

I'm lying on my stomach in bed, where I can see the TV set up in the middle of the room, but my eyes are glued to the small screen in my hand. The dots start and stop twice before the message appears.

> Beau: *Yeah. I have a campus job.*
>
> Me: *I still think if you really wanted to date, you could. We've been texting for . . . almost thirty minutes. That's enough time to grab a coffee or slip into a dark corner of the library for some under-the-shirt action.*
>
> Beau: *Damn, you're right. Gotta go. I have chicks to caffeinate and feel up.*
>
> Me: *I sense you're mocking me, but I should probably encourage it for the sake of the girls at your school.*
>
> Beau: *I don't follow.*
>
> Me: *You're hot.*
>
> Beau: *Earlier I was just 'attractive.'*
>
> Me: *I didn't want it to go to your head.*
>
> Beau: *Too late. I'm screaming it down the hall of my dorm.*

I laugh softly and Holly looks over with a grin. "I'm going to sleep. Do you need the light on?"

"No, I'm good."

"That looks like the beginning of more than a little flirty

texting," she says as she turns off the TV and then all the lights, except the ones casting the room in a festive vibe.

The next afternoon, I text Beau as I'm grabbing lunch.

> Me: How was your test?
>
> Beau: I passed, I think. Did you sleep past your first class?
>
> Me: No, but I wanted to. I still can't believe we texted until 3!
>
> Beau: Me neither. I'm on my second energy drink of the day. How many do you think is too many?
>
> Me: 1 is too many. Those things are awful for you.
>
> Beau: Awful, but currently keeping my eyes open.
>
> Me: I can't remember the last time I had so much fun texting.
>
> Beau: Same. I'm getting ready for work. Text ya later?
>
> Me: Looking forward to it.

And the next day, we're still texting.

> Beau: Favorite food?
>
> Me: Cheeseburger. You?
>
> Beau: Cheeseburger is pretty hard to beat. Add bacon and some jalapenos . . . *drool face*

Me: Do you need a moment alone with your spicy, bacon cheeseburger to show her a good time?

Beau: I need a whole afternoon. Maybe part of the evening, too.

I'm grinning like a fool as Holly and I walk to our afternoon English class.

"You two have been texting nonstop." She elbows me and gives me a look as if to say, 'I told you so.'

"He's funny." I hand over my phone to let her read the last few texts.

She huffs a small laugh. "Sounds like he's an early finisher or maybe he's suffering from performance anxiety."

"That's hilarious," I say as she passes it back. I quickly tap out my sister's response and send it to him as we enter the classroom. Holly loves English and insists on sitting in the front row, so I slide my phone into my backpack, grab a notebook and pen, and lean back in my chair as the professor begins.

Reading and writing are Holly's thing. When we were younger, she would pick out books from the library, devour them, and then pass them on to me. I would slog through, some of them I even really enjoyed, so we could talk about the characters and story lines. We shared everything. If one of us liked something, the other did too. Holly wanted to read every single book in the school library, so I flipped through all of them too. I wanted to do softball, so Holly signed up and stood way out in right field, praying for the ball not to come to her.

Sometime around middle school, we stopped trying to be the same person and found our own interests. I joined more sports, and she signed up for student council. Through it all, we've remained each other's biggest cheerleader and best friend.

And sometimes best friends have to sit in the front row of the class they'd like to sleep through.

131

Except today, I am wide awake. Sleepy, yes, but even if I laid my head down on my pillow, I know sleep wouldn't come.

My skin buzzes and my mind reels. I have the ridiculous urge to doodle hearts on my paper and I find myself smiling as the professor talks about "The Yellow Wallpaper" (and that is not a happy, smiley story).

I'm lost in daydreams and time ticks by faster than usual. When the class is over, Holly looks over at me with a grin. "That was fun."

Nodding, I slide my notebook and pen into my backpack and then retrieve my phone to see Beau's response to my earlier text.

Beau: No, I'd just want to be very, very thorough.

My cheeks are warm and another giddy smile pulls at my lips. "Stell?"

I glance up to find my sister staring at me, brows raised. "Sorry, what?"

She chuckles softly. "I asked if you wanted to go out tonight. The girls across the hall invited us to The Hideout for dinner and then I thought we could stop by Felix's house."

Felix is always having people over and we usually stop by. It's nice to have him at the same school and his teammates and friends are a good group of guys—most of them anyway.

"Swim practice will probably go late. Go to dinner with them and I'll text when I'm done and maybe meet up."

"All right." She takes a step away from me. Our next class isn't together. "Have a good afternoon."

"You too." I loop my backpack around one shoulder and head off in the other direction.

I have two more classes and no time to text Beau during either. In my fitness and sports class, we go to the campus driving range to hit golf balls, and then I have an art class, where I struggle to draw a stack of books.

Holly has already decided to major in English with an

emphasis on creative writing. I'm still undecided. I was considering interior design, but I may pull my hair out if every art pre-requisite (and there are a lot) is this painful.

As I walk to the aquatic center for practice, I still have that buzzing, giddy feeling. I swipe my student athlete ID to get into our training area.

I'm staring down at my phone, rereading Beau's texts, when a quiet whistling catches my attention. At first, I think it's Eric, but when I look up, I spot one of the assistant coaches. He nods and smiles as he passes.

> *Me: Can you whistle?*
>
> *Beau: Sure. Can't everyone.*
>
> *Me: I can't. At least not very well. Do you whistle?*
>
> *Beau: Not on the regular, but occasionally. Why? Deciding we can't be friends now?*
>
> *Me: It is a hard limit for me. I'm going to have to start asking guys on the first date.*
>
> *Beau: Eh. All else fails, you can kiss him to shut him up. I hear that works.* 😏

And just like that I'm thinking about kissing Beau.

Chapter Five

Beau

ON WEDNESDAY NIGHT, I HEAD OVER TO A TEAMMATE'S off-campus house with the rest of the guys. A lot of students went home for the long weekend, but anyone who didn't is ready to cut loose.

We have an early open practice tomorrow. Family members that are in town for Thanksgiving can come by and watch us, and then there's a luncheon for everyone. It's a nice way to make sure everyone gets to have a holiday meal because a lot of guys have families too far away to make it.

My mom and dad flew in earlier tonight. We did the team dinner and then they went back to the hotel to crash. My skin itches from the small interaction. Football is everything to Beau Ricci Sr. I come from a long line of football players. My grandpa led his team to a state championship in high school. My dad and his three brothers all wore a jersey, but none of them went on to play college ball. My dad had a shot, but then blew out his knee his last year of high school.

From an early age, football was this magical, almost religious thing my family did and expected me to continue. At get-togethers, we'd hurry through the meal to get a game going. There's more anticipation for Super Bowl Sunday than Christmas.

I've always enjoyed playing. I like the mental and physical

challenge, and the stability it's brought to my life. When I was having a bad day, my dad would pick up the football and we'd work it out by tossing it back and forth until I couldn't remember what it was that had me down. Work it out on the field, that's our motto. We aren't a family that talks things out; we solve problems with sweat.

I didn't question it when I was younger. It was in my blood. Riccis play football. But ever since I got to college, it's started to feel like the hopes and dreams of every man in my family are resting on my shoulders.

Every game is another opportunity for me to hear how I'm screwing it all up. All my dad could talk about tonight was how my performance this season wasn't going to cut it in the NFL.

I love football, but I have no idea if I have what it takes to play professionally or if that's even what I want. I know I can't imagine listening to him critique every game I play for the rest of my life. He rides my ass harder than my coaches. He's already sent a text with bullet points from dinner. You know, in case I didn't hear him the first time.

"Ricci! You made it." Aaron lifts his chin in acknowledgement as I walk into the living room where several of my teammates are sitting around, beers in hand. A group of girls are huddled up on the couch, whispering and giggling.

"Hey." I lift a hand and let my gaze roam around the room in a hello to everyone.

"Heads up," someone yells, and a beer is tossed in my direction.

I catch it in one hand and take a seat in a wooden chair that's been moved from the dining room for extra seating. "Thanks."

The guys are playing video games, so I crack open the cold beer and lean back to watch. As soon as the cold liquid trickles down my throat, I feel the tension from dinner start to fade. After dealing with my dad, I need to tackle someone on the football field or numb my senses a bit.

Jenny, a girl I made out with one drunken night after a game,

135

stands from where she was sitting on the couch with her friends and comes toward me.

"Hey, Beau. I texted you. Is your phone still broken?"

Aaron coughs and nearly spits out his beer.

"Sorry," he tries to get himself under control. "Wrong pipe."

"I've been busy," I tell her. Not untrue, but could I have found time to hit her back? Considering how many texts I've exchanged with Stella in the past few days, I think the answer to that is definitely yes.

She rolls her eyes, laughs, and plops in my lap before I realize what she's doing. "How do you feel about beer pong?"

"I feel great about it." I lift her off me and then stand. I grab another beer from the kitchen for later and jog down the stairs after her.

We join some buddies just starting a new game. My muscles relax as I concentrate on sinking the ball into the other team's cups. The music is a nice distraction too, so loud it's hard to carry a conversation.

My phone buzzes in my pocket. I groan, assuming it's my dad texting with another critique or fifteen but am pleasantly surprised when I see the message is from someone I want to talk to.

> **Stella: Guess what?!**

One side of my mouth quirks up.

> **Me: You won the lottery?**
>
> **Stella: I wish, but no.**
>
> **Me: Aced a test?**
>
> **Stella: Even better than that.**
>
> **Me: Took a five-hour nap, woke up and had a cheeseburger.**
>
> **Me: No, TWO cheeseburgers.**

Stella: Well, now I'm hungry, but no.

Me: I'm out of guesses. What amazing thing happened to you?

Me: Wait. You met a guy?

A hint of jealousy pulses through me in beat with the music.

Stella: No. I was named athlete of the month at Valley U! I got a fancy plaque with my name on it and everything.

She sends along a picture of herself holding up the plaque. Damn. She's even more gorgeous than I remember.

"Do you want to come with me and some friends to Sigma?" Jenny makes her way in front of me and looks up at me with big, blue eyes.

I slide my phone back in my pocket. "For what?"

She giggles. "To keep hanging out, silly."

Do I? A hint of annoyance still thrums through me. How many more beers is it going to take?

"Beau?" Her brows pull together as she stares at me, waiting for an answer.

"Nah. I don't think so."

"Come on." She sticks out her bottom lip in a pout.

I shake my head.

"What if we go back to my place instead?"

"No thanks. I think I'm going to call it an early night."

"You?"

"Yep."

"Don't be silly. It's early. Come on." She wraps an arm around my bicep and tugs.

I don't know if it's her inability to hear the word no or lingering frustration from the encounter with my dad earlier, but I feel like I'm going to explode. And I guess since I have whistling on the brain, that's what I do.

I'm a little rusty, but I manage to get out a little sound.

Jenny's head tilts and jaw drops, like she isn't sure what to say or do. So, I keep whistling. I raise my brows and step around her. I guess it *is* annoying.

I let my buddies know I'm out for the next game and weave around the downstairs, avoiding Jenny (though I'm prepared to start whistling again if needed), and then head back upstairs.

Off the kitchen is a small balcony. I step out and pull my phone from my pocket. I'm tapping out a reply to Stella's last text when my phone rings with a FaceTime call. *Stella.* I am taken aback, but my adrenaline's pumping.

I accept the call and bring the phone in front of my face. "Hey."

Stella appears, eyes wide. "Oh my god. I'm so sorry. I did not mean to call you."

She disappears, and the camera flips, so I'm seeing the floor and what I assume are Stella's bare feet. There's faint noise in the background. Maybe a TV.

"I'm gonna hang up now."

"Wait! Don't hang up. I'm glad you called."

"You are?"

"Yeah. I was just about to text you, but this is easier."

There's some rustling and then the camera flips again.

"Hey," I say, taking in her wet hair and bare shoulders, the tentative smile on her lips.

"Hi. I am so embarrassed. I just got out of the shower." She tips the phone to show me the top of the blue, fluffy towel wrapped around her. "Where are you?"

"Some of my team—" I start and then catch myself. "A house party off-campus. Congrats on athlete of the month. That's huge."

I lean against the railing, smiling at the girl I've been talking to nonstop since this weekend. And for the first time all night, I don't want to punch a wall.

"Thanks." She beams at me.

"What are you up to tonight? Getting ready to go out?"

"No. I don't think so. Holly went out with a couple of girls on our floor, but I had a late practice, and my parents will be here tomorrow morning for the football game. I'm just not feeling it tonight. One second. I need both hands to get dressed."

"Actually, I'm just about to head out. I'm not really feeling it tonight either. Can I call you back when I get to my dorm?"

"Yeah." She hits me with a smile that has my heart rate picking up speed.

It only takes seven minutes to walk home. I pull on sweats and a T-shirt before calling Stella back.

This time when she appears, the hesitant smile is gone. "Look what I have."

She lifts up a cheeseburger in one hand that makes my stomach growl. "Oh, that looks good."

"It is." She makes a big show of taking a bite and chewing. Her eyes fall closed, and she moans. A moan that goes straight to my dick.

She finishes chewing and asks, "How was the party?"

I clear my throat. "Fine."

"So fine you ditched it early? Is everything okay?"

"Long day," I admit. "I should thank your ex, though."

"My ex?"

"Yeah. I used his trick."

"I don't follow." Her brown eyes squint at me.

I tell her the story of how I whistled until Jenny was uncomfortable and confused.

"You didn't."

"She wasn't taking no for an answer, and I was getting annoyed."

Stella covers her mouth with a hand as she laughs. "That's hilarious. Is this Jenny chick an ex?"

"Not exactly. We made out. Once. I'm not really interested in dating anyone right now."

"Right. You don't have time." She uses air quotes, throwing my words back at me.

139

"It's true. Football takes up so much of my time—" I stop abruptly, the end of the sentence hanging between us. My face goes hot. Ah shit. I wanted to tell her, but not like this.

"Did you say football?" she asks the question slowly, like she isn't sure she heard me right.

"Don't freak out."

"Why would I freak out?" Stella sits a little straighter, and I swear I can see the stoic mask pulling down over her features.

"I play football at Colorado."

"Why would you not tell me that?"

"I'm also from Arizona originally. I went to Rochester High School."

"I know that school. It's not far from where I went." Her tone is somewhere between confused and surprised.

"Yeah." I swallow around a lump the size of a golf ball. "We played your school."

Realization dawns. I can see it the second it happens. All the sass and playfulness that I've come to expect from Stella is gone. "You know Felix."

"Yeah. We've been playing against each other since we were kids."

I hate the hurt in her voice when she says, "You acted like you had no idea who I was."

"I didn't at first. Not until you told me your name. I hoped it was a weird coincidence, but after you ran to your flight, I looked you up."

"That was days ago. Why didn't you tell me? I feel like such an idiot."

"I should have told you. I wanted to, but then I thought it might make things weird. I'm sorry."

"I don't care that you play football."

"Okay."

"I'm serious. Who cares?"

"You might not, but your brother won't like it. We've had a rivalry for years. He is not my biggest fan."

"Look, no offense, but Felix has a lot of guys gunning to beat him. He probably doesn't even know who you are."

I could almost laugh, it's so preposterous. "Oh, he knows."

"Are you any good?"

"Yeah. I'm good."

She gives her head a shake, making the red strands catch the light. "Are you sure? I didn't have you pegged as a football player."

"You want proof?"

She nods.

I stand and take the phone with me, flipping the camera to show her my bag on the floor. I scrounge around until I find a smelly practice jersey, tape, gloves, and some eye black.

"I probably have a cup in here somewhere too if you want to see that."

"No." She sighs. "I believe you. You're either a football player or really committed to the lie."

"And?"

Another big sigh puffs out her cheeks. "I don't know."

Chapter Six

Stella

"I CAN'T BELIEVE YOU USED TO GO THERE FOR VACATION every year too. We were probably there at the same time." I cover a yawn.

"Probably," Beau says. He's lying in his bed in the dark, the screen of his phone providing the smallest bit of light for me to see him. We've been talking for three hours. Topics have included everything from class schedules to family vacations. The only thing we haven't talked about is him being a football player. A football player my brother hates, apparently.

Holly is still out, but Beau's roommate, who's also a football player, came back and crashed thirty minutes ago. He has ear buds in now and his voice is quiet as he speaks. "Actually, nah, I would have tried to hit on you."

"Or my sister," I say, "since we look identical."

"You look that much alike?"

"I think you maybe don't understand how *identical* twins work."

"Okay, smart ass." His mouth twists into a playful smirk. "Those dudes from the show *Selling Sunset* are twins and they look different."

"Hold up, did you just admit to watching *Selling Sunset*?" My cheeks hurt from grinning so much.

"I admitted no such thing. I merely confessed to knowing the show has twins on it. And that one of them dated Chrishell, but they broke up because he wasn't ready for kids, and she was. It was a real tearjerker."

Laughter escapes my lips. "You *so* watch it. Oh man, I don't know if I can keep talking to you with that knowledge."

"It's a little drama-filled for my tastes, but the real estate is pretty incredible. Plus, the cars."

"That is such a guy reason to watch." I turn over on my side and place the phone on the bed, so I can still see it while lying down. "People that know us well can tell Holly and me apart. Our styles are different. She loves shoes and accessories, and I'm more casual. She's quieter than me too."

"Have you ever pulled the switcheroo on a guy?"

"No, but once in high school, the guy I was dating grabbed her ass because he got us mixed up. And another time, a guy asked me out, but thought he was asking out Holly."

"Still, seems like it'd be cool to have a twin."

"I can't imagine it any other way." I shrug and then we fall quiet. I know he needs to go. He has practice in the morning and his family is in town, but it feels like as soon as we get off the phone, the reality of the situation is going to set in.

He's my brother's rival. Can this really go anywhere? Do I even want it to? I know that I really enjoy talking to him.

"I have an idea," I say, sitting up and bringing the phone closer to my face.

"What's that?"

"What if we kept talking?"

"I'd probably fall asleep eventually."

"You're so funny." I laugh, quick and light, but my nerves kick up as I continue, "Seriously, though, what can it hurt? You're a million miles away anyway."

"Or a thousand."

"That might as well be a million with our schedules. It isn't like we can see each other or date, or whatever." My face goes a little hot.

One side of his mouth lifts. "Did you just admit you would want to date me if I lived close?"

"I admitted no such thing," I say, stealing his words from earlier. "Besides you're too busy." I think back to everything he's told me. "Wait, your job."

"I was talking about football," he admits. "Still want to keep talking to me?"

"Yes. Though, I think we have to redo every conversation we've had."

He crooks an arm behind his head. "I've got time for that."

"You are kind of fun to talk to."

"Right back at ya."

"So, friends?" I ask.

"You're sure?" The uneasy expression on his face makes me doubt myself.

I love my brother. We're a lot alike, both athletic and competitive, so I'd like to think I can put myself in his shoes in this situation. How would I feel if he dated a diver from another college? I'd probably be slightly annoyed, but Beau and I aren't even talking about dating. We're friends. Barely even friends, really, since we've just texted. (And had one three-hour, make that four now, phone call.) I'm sure it's just the excitement of talking to someone new, and in a week or two, we'll have run out of things to talk about.

And if we don't, then I'll tell Felix, and I bet he won't even care. Fingers crossed.

I nod. "Yeah, I'm sure."

Over the next few weeks, Beau and I continue texting. Before classes, during lunch, after swim and football practice, while studying, at parties—we text a lot. He's the first person I talk to every morning, and most nights, I fall asleep texting him. And it's mostly friendly, a little flirty.

I keep waiting for one or both of us to get bored with talking, but I'm less confident that's actually going to happen. I like Beau. I like talking to him.

After a home meet, I check my phone to find a text waiting for me.

> *Beau: Good luck at your meet! Let me know how it goes.*
>
> *Me: First place!*
>
> *Beau: Congrats!*
>
> *Me: Thanks. I heard you won too! Wooo!*
>
> *Beau: Thanks. You should get your sexy ass on a plane and come party with me tonight to celebrate.*
>
> *Me: Be right there. Save me a shot.*
>
> *Beau: I'll save a whole bottle for you.*
>
> *Me: Drunk already?*
>
> *Beau: Not yet, but I'm working on it.*

His team played their final game of the season, so I'm not surprised that he's hitting it hard tonight. And I do wish I could go hang with him instead of going to the swim and dive party I promised my friend Rachel I'd go to with her. I think hanging with Beau would be fun. We've chatted enough after or during parties for me to discern that he's the life of the party, always up for a game of beer pong, and on an exceptionally celebratory night, he breaks out the liquor and does shots instead of beer.

I've also learned from those drunken conversations that things with his family are a little strained. His dad puts a lot of pressure on him with football. At first, it was hard for me to feel sorry for him about it. I'd love for my family to show a little more interest in my diving.

Don't get me wrong, my parents are supportive, but Felix gets most of the attention in that department. Especially since he started getting endorsements. I'm proud of my brother, truly. He's maybe the most supportive person I have outside of Holly. He's quick to talk me up and shine the spotlight on me, but people still smile politely at me and then ask him about football.

I love diving and I don't need people to hype up the sport to be proud of myself and want to continue doing it, but I can't deny that it's irritating when people fawn over Felix and his football games and don't even mention my meets.

All this to say when Beau first grumbled about pressure from his family, I chalked it up as not a big deal. But it's different for him. They nitpick and critique to the point that I think he struggles to enjoy the victories.

When I get to the party, I check to see if he's texted again. He hasn't, so I send another.

> *Me: On a scale of 1-10, how much do you wish I were there?*
>
> *Beau: 11, duh. When girls ask this question, no matter the topic, the correct answer is always 11.*
>
> *Me: A wise ass, as usual.*
>
> *Beau: And a sexy ass, as usual.*

Electricity hums under my skin at the compliment.

> *Beau: Also, my real answer is still 11. What are you doing over break? Maybe we can meet up.*
>
> *Me: You're going to be in Arizona?*
>
> *Beau: Yeah, of course.*

I don't know why I didn't consider this sooner. He's from Arizona. Our parents live maybe forty-five minutes from each other. A new level of excitement rushes through me, but just as quickly, Felix's face flashes in my mind.

Beau's going to be close. So close. But how am I going to see him?

Me: One more day!

Beau: Twenty-one hours and thirty-eight minutes, but who's counting?

Me: LOL. You, apparently. Plans for your holiday break?

Beau: Nah, not really. Hanging with the fam. I might see if some buddies from high school want to head up to Show Low this weekend to ski. You?

Me: Not sure, but skiing sounds fun! I bet you're pretty cute in ski goggles.

Beau: Only one way to find out. Come with.

We never directly talk about Felix, but it's getting harder to avoid. Especially if I want to see Beau over the holiday break. I confirmed their rivalry by casually mentioning I was talking to a guy from Colorado University. The very first words out of my brother's mouth were, "I hate their entire football team."

I slide my phone into my backpack, without answering him, as I walk into the dining hall. Holly is already at our usual table.

"Hey," I say, sitting across from her.

She pushes one of the plates on her tray toward me. "They ran out of blueberry bagels."

"This is perfect. Thank you." I tear off a hunk of the cinnamon bagel in front of me and smile. "Two more classes and we're done! We'll have survived our first semester as college students!"

"Felix already left," Holly says, and then scrunches up her nose. "I hope the house isn't trashed when we get there."

Our parents took advantage of all their children being away at college and finally went on a two-week vacation. They won't be back until Christmas Eve. Felix is house-sitting, which more than likely means he'll be throwing a party every night until they return.

"What if we didn't go home just yet?" I ask, an idea forming.

Holly's wearing a red T-shirt and earrings in the shape of candy canes that dangle as she tilts her head to the side. "You want to stay on campus longer?"

"No. Let's go to the cabin." I don't know why I didn't think of it sooner. Our family has a vacation home in Flagstaff near the ski resort. It's a small two-bedroom without a lot of fancy amenities, but the resort nearby is beautiful, and I can't think of a better way to spend a few days than snowboarding and relaxing with Holly after our first semester of college.

It's been a fun few months, but we have seen a lot less of each other due to our different schedules. And if I'm totally honest, I need a distraction. I can't sit at home knowing Beau is an hour away and not want to do something reckless like see him. He's insistent that Felix will freak out, which has me freaking out.

Holly is quiet as she considers my proposal. "By ourselves? We've never gone just the two of us."

"Exactly. I think it'll be fun. I miss you."

She laughs softly. "You see me every day."

"I know, but we're both busy. It's not the same."

"Yeah," she agrees. "Okay."

I squeal and clap my hands.

"But only if we can still do all our usual holiday traditions. I'm so bummed Mom and Dad are going to be gone until next week. We're going to miss out on baking cookies, decorating gingerbread houses, putting up a tree . . ." she trails off.

"Of course. We can do all that. Or as much as we can fit in a weekend."

"All right, yeah. I'm in." Her smile is filled with the same excitement I feel. "How's Beau? Any plans to see each other over break?"

I can't be sure, but I think my face turns red. Holly still doesn't know that Beau plays football, but she knows we've been talking nonstop these past few weeks and that he is from Arizona, not far from where we grew up.

"No. I don't think so. He has a bunch of family stuff going on." I wave off her question and stuff another bite of bagel in my mouth.

"Too bad," she says, "I'd like to meet this mystery guy you're talking to all day, every day."

"We're just friends and it's not *all* day," I say at the same time my phone pings in my backpack. I reach for it, smiling when I see the text, a photo of Beau in ski goggles. His hair is sticking out everywhere, one brow is cocked, and he has a flirty smirk.

Holly laughs. "I think you just made my point for me."

Beau has a big, final group project due tomorrow before he's done for the semester, so we can't talk on the phone. Instead, I'm packing and cleaning up my side of the room while Holly is across the hall, helping our neighbor with an English paper.

> **Beau: I hate group projects. <expletive smiley>**
>
> **Me: You've mentioned that once or twice before.**

He's said it about a hundred times today alone.

> **Beau: Three of the five people in our group totally flaked.**
>
> **Me: So not cool.**

I snap a picture of me in a pair of old sunglasses I find in the bottom of my closet and send it to him. He sends back a photo of him, staring blankly at the camera, scratching the side of his face with his middle finger. Even not trying, he's ridiculously handsome.

I stare at the picture longer than a friend should. He's in the library. I know because he told me that's where they were meeting, and because I can see the shelves of books in the background. I can just make out the arm and leg of the person sitting next to him. A girl. And irrational jealousy flares inside me.

Me: Is the girl next to you one of the flakes?

Beau: Nah, Paige is cool. We sent everyone else away and we're just going to stay here all night until we bang it out.

Me: Fuuuun.

Bang it out? My face is on fire. I know he probably doesn't mean they're literally going to bang it out, but he could be hooking up with other girls. No, it can't be *other* girls because I'm *not* his girl. We're friends. He could be hooking up with girls. Because that's what hot college guys do.

I bring the sleeve of a sweatshirt hanging in my closet to my face and scream into it.

"Everything okay?" Holly's voice makes me jump.

"Yep." I step back. "Just trying to organize this disaster of a closet. Are you done?"

"No, I just came back for a book." She grabs a paperback from a stack next to her desk. "I'm lending it to Alexis over break."

"Did you write your name in it?" I tease. Holly is very protective of her books.

"No," she says defensively and then lowers her voice, "I didn't love this one."

With a smile, she disappears back into the hallway.

I resist the overwhelming urge to text Beau and instead pull every single item out of my closet. I refold and carefully hang items all facing the same direction. I even line up my shoes at the bottom. In other words, I'm going out of my mind thinking about Beau hooking up with his hot study partner.

When my phone finally pings again, two hours later, I scramble up off the floor and snatch it from under a pile of clean towels.

Beau: DONE!

Me: All banged out?

Beau: Yeah, freaking exhausted.

Me: I'll bet. Banging is tiring.

The three little dots start and stop, there's a pause, and then they start again. My heart races.

Beau: Especially when it's several hours long.

He's being cute and flirty, but I can't concentrate until I know if he banged Paige or not. Maybe I've been imagining this thing between us as something more than it is. I decide to go with direct.

Me: She must have been amazing. <high five emoji>

Okay, so not exactly direct. My phone rings a minute later with a FaceTime request. I run my hand over my ponytail and then smile. "Hey."

"Hey." His voice is low and gravelly. He sounds tired. It's dark outside as he walks through campus toward his dorm. I've never been to the Colorado campus, but I feel like I have the path to his dorm memorized from the buildings and trees in the background.

"Heading back to your dorm?"

"Yeah. We just finished."

"Cool." It's the first time I've felt like I don't know what to say to Beau. Even in the beginning, we were never at a loss for words.

"You know I didn't really bang a girl in the library, right? Even I'm not that smooth."

I laugh, but it comes out stiff and brittle. "Hey, it could be worse. It could have been the dining hall or the computer lab. I swear I walked in on two guys seconds from tearing each other's clothes off one time. I can't bring myself to use public computers anymore without sanitizing the keyboard and mouse first. And don't even get me started on people who make out in the—"

"Stella?"

"Yeah." I take a big breath and let it out slowly.

"You're acting weird. I didn't have sex with her."

"Oh. Okay."

He stops walking, a light from somewhere shining across his face. His brows tug together and his mouth is in a flat, serious line. "Wait. Are you jealous?"

"What?" The single word comes out high-pitched. "No, of course not."

He chuckles. "I think you are and it's sexy as hell."

"It is?"

"Yeah. Hot girls not wanting other girls to touch me is suuu-per sexy."

"But you don't date."

"Even still, it's sexy."

"Fine. I was jealous," I admit.

"Wanna know a secret?"

"Always."

"Every time you mention that prick ex-boyfriend, I want to pummel his face."

"You're jealous of Eric?"

He shrugs.

"You're right. It is sexy."

"I like you. I thought that was obvious."

"I know you like me as a friend," I say.

"You think I talk to my friends this much?"

"I don't know," I say, and then. "No."

"I like you, Stella. I'm not hooking up or even talking to other girls right now."

"You're not?"

"No." He pauses. "I guess we've been talking so much I haven't thought about it."

"Yeah." My pulse races. "We have been talking a lot."

His mouth pulls into a playful smile and he starts walking again. "This is when you say, 'I'm not hooking up with other guys either.' Unless you are and then forget everything I just said."

"I'm not," I say through a giggle. "I like you too."

Saying the words has a new kind of anxiety hitting me. "Now what?"

"I don't know. I've never been in this position before."

"You've never dated someone at another college?"

"Or at any college, but that isn't what I meant. I meant I've never liked a girl whose family hates me."

"I'll talk to Felix over break. He's always been supportive of my relationships."

"This is different."

"He just needs a chance to get to know you. Who could possibly hate you? You're so sweet and handsome."

"Felix is into girls, yeah?" He questions with a small smirk.

"Yeah. Why?"

"Then I don't think the fact that I'm sweet and handsome is going to win me any favors with him."

"It'll be fine," I say, a new sense of hope surging inside of me with the words. "You'll see."

Chapter Seven

Beau

Stella: OMG. I don't know how you pulled this off but THANK YOU!

I GRIN DOWN AT MY PHONE, THE PICTURE OF HER WITH THE giant cheeseburger I DoorDashed to her dorm filling up my screen. I even got the delivery driver to put a Christmas bow on top.

Me: Merry Christmas, Stella. I hope you have a great holiday break.

Stella: I'll text you when we get to the cabin. Have a safe flight! Don't talk to any cute girls in the airport. They're probably crazy and will ramble on about their ex-boyfriends.

Me: The only thing I'm going to be doing in the airport is sleeping. Someone kept me up last night.

Stella: <angel emoji>

We're both heading home for the break. Me to a family that probably can't wait to tell me all the reasons our team didn't make it to a bowl game this year, and Stella to hers, with Felix. She said we could still talk, but she's sidestepped any attempt I've made to make plans to see each other.

I slide my phone into my pocket as I walk out of the airport. The Arizona heat hits me, and I inhale. I missed this. It was snowing in Colorado this morning and barely above freezing. A few weeks of sun and warm weather is going to be nice.

My mom's car is parked along the curb and my dad stands at the back next to the popped trunk.

"I see him," my mom says, loud enough her voice carries up the busy sidewalk. I lift a hand in a wave and then start for them.

Dad meets me halfway and pulls me into a bear hug. "There he is."

"Hey, Dad."

He lets go and takes a long look at me. "You look like you shrunk in the three weeks since I've seen you, kid. I hope you didn't stop working out just because the season is over. This is when you need to make gains."

I bite back a retort. Mom comes over and hugs me, holding on a little longer than Dad did. She pulls back almost reluctantly. "We better get you home. Everyone is waiting to see you."

"Who?"

"Your aunts and uncles, Grandpa John, everyone."

"They're already at the house?"

"Of course." Dad's mouth pulls into a broad smile.

The fifteen-minute drive to my parents' house passes too quickly. Cars line the driveway and curb, and as soon as I step out of the car, I can hear voices and laughter in the backyard.

"Heads up," someone yells.

I drop my bag in time to catch the football sailing toward the car.

"Touchdown!" Uncle Terry's arms are raised over his head, and he wears that same broad smile my dad does.

"Hey, Uncle T."

He closes the distance between us, hugs me, lifting me off the ground and shaking me. Uncle Terry is six foot five and as wide as a doorway. He still looks like the defensive tackle he once was.

"They feeding you in Colorado, boy?"

"Yeah." I catch my breath as he sets me back down. "They're definitely feeding me. Maybe you could miss a meal or two." I poke at his stomach, which is hard and muscular, but it still eggs him on. Uncle Terry gives me the same shit my dad does, but it's easier to take from him for some reason.

He takes the football still clutched to my side and extends it, using it to point at me. "You'll wish you had a little more meat on your bones when I'm taking you to the ground."

"Let him at least put his stuff away." Mom takes the football from him. "Are the burgers and steaks done?"

"Working on it." Uncle Terry flashes another smile. "About five more minutes."

Mom nods and barks out orders like a drill sergeant. "Lunch, cleanup, *then* football."

"Yes, dear." Dad kisses her on the cheek.

I get a few minutes to myself while I take my bags to my old bedroom. My gaze falls over the bookcase filled with paperbacks and football trophies. I grab the worn football from my desk and sit on the end of my bed, then fall back and stare up at the ceiling.

Letting out a long breath, I fight to suppress the feelings of resentment. My family is all here to welcome me home. They're proud of me, I know that. But what I really want is a few weeks where I don't have to think about football at all.

After lunch, where I'm peppered with questions about the season and when practices start again, followed by cleanup, and a game of football, everyone finally leaves. Dad falls asleep in the recliner and Mom heads out to grocery shop. I take my phone outside. Stella sent a couple of texts during the day. She and Holly were going to their family's cabin for the weekend, and from the selfie she sent, snow in the background, I'd say they made it.

> *Me: Brrr. That looks cold.*
>
> *Stella: I love the snow!*
>
> *Me: Me too, but I've missed the sun and warm weather. Done any skiing yet?*
>
> *Stella: No. Hopefully tomorrow. Are you going to Show Low?*

Instead of texting again, I call.

"Hey," she answers on the second ring. The background is noisy, and I can barely hear her next words. "One second. I'm moving somewhere quieter."

"If you guys are out somewhere, you can call me later."

"No," she says, "we aren't out. My brother and his teammates had the same idea that Holly and I did."

"They're at the cabin?"

"Yep."

"I thought Felix was house-sitting."

"So did I. I guess he went there first and is planning to go back in a few days to check on things."

A knot forms in my stomach and I'm quiet.

"Is it weird?" she asks, reading my mind.

It shouldn't be. I've known that Felix was her brother all along, and it isn't like us talking when he's nearby is any better or worse than when he isn't, but it still has unease prickling up my spine.

"It's weird. I know. It is for me too," she says, before I find my nerve to say as much. Her voice sounds cheerier when she asks, "How's home?"

"Good. The whole fam came over for lunch."

"I love how close you are with your extended family. Both of my parents are only children, so we don't have any cousins."

"Yeah, they're great."

"You sound tired. Everything okay?"

"Yeah."

"Liar."

I chuckle. "I was hoping for a break from football, but it's all they want to talk about and do. I don't want to seem ungrateful. I know they're being supportive, and I feel like a dick for it annoying me."

"You aren't a dick."

I don't feel as confident in that assessment.

"What are you doing tonight?" she asks. "You didn't answer my question about Show Low. When do you leave?"

"That got postponed until next weekend, but a few high school buddies are going out tonight. I think I might stop by for a bit."

"That sounds fun."

"What about you?"

"I think we're staying at the cabin. The guys stocked the fridge with beer and there's enough liquor for the entire neighborhood. Wish you could come."

"Yeah. Me too."

"I'm going to talk to him over break. Felix, I mean."

"Stell," I start.

"I know, I know. He hates you, yadda, yadda. But are you sure? Maybe he just hates your team."

I stay silent. I wish that were the case, but know it isn't.

"This is silly. I like you, you like me, you both play football, who cares?" I can practically see her brown eyes rolling and her hand waving in the air as she talks. "I'm going to tell him right now."

She moves closer to the noise again.

"Wait, Stell. I don't know if that's a good idea."

"Do you want to see me over break?"

"Of course, I do, but maybe wait until the entire team isn't around." I chuckle loose the knot in my chest.

"Oh, right. Good call." She huffs. "It's frustrating, knowing you're so close and going to parties with girls that aren't me."

"You're sexy when you're jealous."

She growls.

"Well, I'd invite you here, but tomorrow we're going to the Cardinals game, and pretty much every day next week is going to be filled with helping my dad build a she-shed for my mom."

"A she-shed, seriously?"

"Oh yeah, she said she wants a place she can make as girly as she wants and put all her collectibles where they won't get broken."

"Your family sounds rowdy."

"They are." A rough chuckle escapes. "They're great though, really."

"I know. I get that you can be annoyed and still love them. Trust me. That's not unique to your family."

"Yeah, you're right."

"Of course, I am. Now go get ready and meet up with your friends, then send me drunk texts later."

"All right. I can do that." Talking to her, even seeing her face, doesn't feel like enough anymore. I wish she were here, that I could reach out and touch her. "Thanks, Stella."

"For what?"

"I don't know. Talking to you always makes me feel better. You get me. It's . . . nice."

"Right back at ya."

Chapter Eight

Stella

THE COLD STINGS MY FACE. I CATCH MY BREATH, dragging the crisp, mountain air into my lungs at the bottom of the ski trail. It's our second day at the cabin in Flagstaff. What I had hoped would be a nice, quiet weekend with my sister is more like an endless football team party with a winter backdrop.

Six of us crammed into the small, two-bedroom cabin is comical. But watching Holly and Teddy circle each other, like maybe the two of them might actually admit their feelings to one another, has made it totally worth it. I have all my fingers and toes crossed for that. Talking with Beau every day, all day, might have turned me into a romantic. I want Holly to feel the same way I am.

Felix stops next to me, spraying me with snow. He lifts his goggles to the top of his head. Lucas, Emmett, and Teddy are right behind him. "We're going to head in and warm up, grab something to drink."

"Good idea," I say. "I forgot how cold it gets up here."

I brought my ski pants, coat, gloves, hat—the usual, but I need more warm layers. I'm not used to the cold from living in perpetual summertime my entire life.

Holly came with us today, but stayed in the lodge to read and hang out. She's curled up in a chair next to the floor-to-ceiling windows that look out onto the mountain, a book in her lap. Felix and the guys are slower to peel off their gear, and I'm the first to plop down in the chair in front of her.

"I missed this place." I glance around at the holiday decorations inside the lodge—a giant Christmas tree, the roaring fireplace with garland hung above it, and elegant wreaths with red and green bows expertly placed throughout the space. It's the kind of holiday vibe that feels like you're in a movie.

"Me too," she says as she looks up from the pages, blinking several times like she was lost in the fictional world.

"Already on your second book?" She brought two for the day at the lodge. Reading is her sport.

"Yeah," she says as Felix and Teddy join us. Teddy takes off his coat and gloves, and then rubs his hands in front of him. The big, lovable guy did as much falling as skiing. It was his first time, and he should probably stick to football, or at least bring his pads next time.

"I need to dry off," he says as he takes a seat.

"You only get wet if you fall." Felix grins. "I'm gonna get a drink. Want anything?"

"Nah." Teddy sneaks another glance at my sister. These two are freaking adorable but also infuriating. The vibes between them are ridiculous. Just kiss each other already.

I bring a hand to my mouth, wondering, not for the first time, what it'd be like to kiss Beau. It's weird not seeing him in person, not being able to touch him, kiss him, but it's also allowed me to really get to know him.

"I'll come with you." I get to my feet to go with Felix. Holly's eyes widen, as if being stuck with her crush is a real inconvenience. I know she stresses about saying or doing the wrong thing, but I don't think that's possible when it comes to Teddy. "I need something hot. I'm frozen to the bone. I should have packed warmer clothes."

Emmett and Lucas are talking to a couple of girls on the far side of the bar, while Felix and I take a seat a few chairs down.

"Man, I missed this place." Felix rests his elbows on the bar.

"I was just saying the same thing to Holly. What has it been? Two years since we were here?"

"Yeah." He nods. "I think so. The year before I left for college."

The bartender comes over to take our order. I get a hot chocolate and Felix gets coffee. We linger at the bar as we take the first sips. Warmth spreads through me as I drink the hot liquid.

"I'm sorry we ruined your plans to hang at the cabin and have a chill weekend, but it's cool to see you." He nudges me with an elbow. "I see you almost every week, but it never feels like we have time to talk."

"Yeah," I agree. "And it's not so bad having you guys around."

One side of his mouth lifts in a smile. "How's diving going? That idiot ex-boyfriend come groveling back yet?"

"Diving is good, and definitely not. He's still dating that girl on my team."

"Ouch." Felix's face twists with his displeasure. "I'm sorry. That has to suck."

"Actually, not really. Not anymore. I told you I met someone."

"The guy from the airport?" His brows lift. "You're still texting? I figured that was already over."

Nodding, I push down the apprehension that's kept me from telling Felix a lot of the details. "He's really cool. I think you'd like him."

His head tilts to the side. "I don't know, Stell. What do you really know about this guy? He could be a total loser."

"No. Maybe at first I would have believed that, but we've talked too many times for him to be hiding a psycho alter ego."

"Where's he go to college again?"

I run my finger over the rim of my mug. "Colorado. He's a history major and a gamer. He's into watching speedrunning. You guys have a lot in common, I think."

I feel like I'm championing a bit too hard, telling Felix all the things I know about Beau that will convince my brother to give him a chance, but leaving out the one big thing that could ruin everything.

"His college sucks, but otherwise, he sounds all right."

I roll my eyes. "You think every college sucks besides Valley."

"Nah, that's not true." His head bounces side to side. "Okay, it's a little true. But Colorado's football team is one of the worst. Those guys play dirty. Ask Garrison. He missed most of the season thanks to that fucker, Beau Ricci."

The hairs on the back of my neck rise.

"Beau Ricci?" His name comes out in a whisper. I fight to keep my voice calm and even as I add, "What happened?"

"The guy is a total prick. That's what." Felix shakes his head. "You remember that game when Garrison got hurt?"

I can't find my voice, so I nod.

"That was him. That was Ricci."

Felix's words stick with me all day. I don't want to believe them, but, admittedly, it's having some effect on me because I haven't responded to any of Beau's texts since this morning.

There's another party at our cabin tonight. Felix invited some guys that live local to drive up for the night, and Lucas and Emmett told the girls they met at the resort earlier today. Word spread fast and our living room is packed full of people, most of whom I don't know.

Beau: Hope you're having a good time.

He attached a photo from the Cardinals game he's at. He ditched his glasses and has on a red beanie pulled down low over his ears.

Me: Sorry, long day. We went skiing and now the cabin is filled with people I don't know. I'm about to hide in my bedroom and watch a Christmas movie.

Beau: What's your favorite Christmas movie?

Me: Home Alone 2. You?

Beau: I don't think I've seen that one all the way through.

*Me: *GASP* You think you know a person.*

Beau: I'll add it to the queue this break. I like A Christmas Story.

Me: You'll shoot your eye out!

He replies with a GIF from the movie. My lips pull into a smile as I stare down at the screen. It's so easy between us. I'm giddy just talking about our favorite holiday movies. I feel like we could really have something, and I refuse to give that up over some stupid football rivalry. Felix has to be wrong about him.

Me: I want to see you over break.

Beau: Same.

Me: Then let's do it.

The dots start and stop.

Beau: Are you sure?

Me: Positive.

Chapter Nine

Beau

I SPEND THE WEEKEND HELPING MY DAD WITH MY MOM'S she-shed and hitting up local parties. On Wednesday night, almost a week since I've been home, I find myself sitting at another house partying, killing an evening while Stella is busy.

"Congrats on the season, man." Lonnie, a buddy and teammate from high school, lifts his beer. "I'm really happy for you. Things seem like they're going well."

"Yeah, they are. What's new with you?" We're sitting in his parents' basement. A small party has formed, mostly old teammates that are home for the holidays from their respective colleges or jobs, a few other classmates, and some people I don't recognize.

"Nothing, really. Aside from classes, I'm working a few hours on campus, and the rest of the time I'm chilling. It's amazing how much more free time I have without football." He chuckles and adds, "I miss it, though, running out onto the field, that rush of adrenaline, the girls. It's a lot easier to pick up chicks in a jersey, I'll tell you that. I bet you are cleaning up at college."

"Eh." I make a non-committal gesture. Before I met Stella? Absolutely.

He looks downright appalled.

"I'm talking to someone. A girl at another school."

"That's awesome. The mighty Beau Ricci has fallen. Now I

understand why we had a record-breaking year for rainfall. Girls from Arizona to Colorado were crying tears of sadness."

I nod, some unfamiliar emotion swirling in my stomach.

"Or not?"

"No, it is. It's complicated. Do you remember Felix Walters?"

"Of course. QB at Newburg High."

"It's his sister, Stella."

"No way." His eyes widen. "That's crazy. I hated Newburg."

"We all did."

He snorts. "I guess those rivalries were kind of dumb. What's Walters like off the field? He cool?"

"I haven't met him yet," I admit, then proceed to tell Lonnie how I ran into Stella at the airport, not knowing who she was.

"Wow!" My old teammate runs a hand over his disheveled red hair. "Small world."

I study him for a beat. "That's all you have to say?"

He shrugs. "What else is there to say?"

"You don't think he'll want to punch my face in?"

"Maybe. I don't know. What does your girl say?"

"She thinks it'll be cool."

"But you're not so sure?"

"I wish I was."

He leans closer and points across the room. "You see that guy in the white hat just walking in?"

I nod. "Yeah."

"Toby Malcolm."

"The kicker for Leewood." Another high school team we battled against every year.

"Me and him got into a fist fight junior year because we both showed up at the same party."

"I remember that. He kicked your ass."

"I got a few good punches in." He puffs out his chest, which makes me laugh.

"And now you're friends? How'd that happen?"

"Yeah. We both go to ASU. We had a class together last semester and I got to know him. He's cool."

The story, however incomparable to things with me and Felix, gives me hope.

"I don't think it's going to be that easy for me."

"Take it from someone who has been away from football for a couple of years, it's not that serious, man."

A laugh escapes my lips.

"Worst case, the guy pops you one and then you're cool."

"And best case?"

"You pop him first." Lonnie winks. "I'm gonna grab another beer. Want anything?"

"No." I shake my head.

My buddy gets up and crosses the room. I watch as he approaches Malcolm and the two slap hands and hug.

Standing, I pull my phone from my pocket and read the last text from Stella. They're going to some party at a ski resort up in Flagstaff tonight. She sent me a photo of her dress options, laid out on a bed. All different colors and styles. All satin and lacy. All short. Damn, I wish I were going to see her all dolled up. I wish I could see her, period.

> Me: *Which dress did you decide on wearing?*
>
> Stella: *Red, I think. I don't know. I've changed like five times.*
>
> Me: *Show me.*

A minute later, she does. I rub at my chest. She's gorgeous, of course, but it's more than that. We've talked a little less during break because we're both busy hanging out with family, and I've missed her. She's become such a big part of my life in the past month and I want more. It's an unfamiliar feeling.

> Me: *You look killer in red. Don't change.*

Stella: You don't even want to see the other options?

"Do I want to see the other options?" I mutter under my breath with a rough chuckle.

Me: Is that really a question?

Me: Of course I want to see the other options, but this is the one.

What follows is a series of sexy selfies that has blood rushing south, which is probably the reason I start for the door.

"Hey, Ricci." Lonnie drapes an arm around my shoulders as I get close. "Meet my new BFF, Toby Malcolm."

I lift my chin. "Hey, man. I remember you."

"Same. I hear you're still playing. Colorado?" he asks.

"Yeah. And you're going to ASU with this clown?" I tilt my head toward Lonnie.

"I'm too drunk to fight you right now, Ricci, but I'll get you this weekend."

"You're going to Show Low, too?" Toby asks.

"Actually, I'm not sure."

Lonnie drops his arm and stares at me, confusion marring his brow, but then a smile slowly lifts the corners of his mouth. "I feel you, Ricci. Hey, you call if you want some backup with Walters."

I laugh. "I think I better do this one on my own, but I appreciate it."

I hold out my hand and he takes it. "If you change your mind, you know where to find us."

Outside in my car, I pull up the ski resort address on my phone. Three hours to get there. Maybe less, if I hurry.

Chapter Ten

Stella

THE RESORT'S HOLIDAY PARTY IS EVERYTHING I HOPED. From the over-the-top decorations to the band set up in the corner playing Christmas music, to Holly and Teddy making eyes at one another. It's been such a great week. We've skied, snowboarded, had an ugly Christmas sweater party, baked cookies, and so much more.

We leave tomorrow and I'm actually disappointed. Although excited about being closer to Beau.

"I'm so happy for you." I lean closer to Holly and whisper the words.

My twin blushes and then shoots another dreamy glance in the direction of her favorite football player. Earlier this week, Felix had to go to Scottsdale to check in on the house and me and Emmett went with him, leaving Holly and Teddy all alone. It took some convincing, though. Holly worried she'd say or do something embarrassing, but I gave her an epic pep talk and she finally agreed to hang back with Teddy for the day.

Then it snowed . . . a lot. We couldn't come back until the next day and, though it wasn't exactly how I envisioned it, leaving them alone did the trick. Holly finally made a move. Hallelujah.

They haven't told Felix yet, which is why they're shooting covert glances at one another and not making out on the spot.

My cell buzzes in my hand. I know, I know. I should put it away, but this whole fun, ritzy, slightly romantic, holiday party, combined with seeing my sister so happy, has me all up in my feelings. I wish Beau were here. I almost broke down and saw him while I was in Scottsdale, but he was busy with his dad and then . . . I don't know, I got nervous.

Beau: How's the party?

Me: It's fun. What are you up to tonight?

"Put that away," Holly nudges me. "You're missing this and it's incredible."

"Okay, okay." I wait a second more to see if Beau responds quickly. When he doesn't, I slide my phone into my purse. "You're right. I've wanted to go to this party for years."

Garrison and James, two more of my brother's teammates, came down for the party tonight. They're standing with Teddy, Lucas and Felix, the five of them shuffling awkwardly next to us. It's a lot of older couples dancing and people our age hanging at the bar. Everyone is dressed up and way more reserved than the parties the guys are used to throwing and attending. I fight a chuckle at the five of them. They look like they don't know what to do with themselves. Except Lucas. He has a playfulness about him that makes me think he probably never feels uncomfortable.

As if proving my thought, he spins onto the dance floor and holds out his hand to me. "Dance, Stella?"

I glance at Holly. "Impressive. You can finally tell us apart."

He holds up his hand. Something is scribbled in ink. He stares at his palm as he reads, "Holly is in green, and Stella is in red."

"Oh my gosh." Laughter bubbles then spills over. "That is truly pathetic."

But a little fun is exactly what I need tonight, so I step toward him and take his hand.

He wraps an arm around my back and moves us to the beat.

"You're not a bad dancer," I tell him.

"I'm a great dancer." His grip loosens and he steps back, then tugs me forward.

Holly and Teddy join us on the dance floor and the rest of the guys head to the bar. Felix stares at his best friend and sister as he walks in the back of the group.

Holly notices and pink dots her cheeks.

They must have told him. *Wow. Go, Holly.*

The four of us dance through two more songs. I'm smiling, but my heart isn't really in it. I should have taken Beau up on his offer to hang out sooner. If Felix can handle his best friend hooking up with his sister, then surely me dating a guy from another team won't be such a big deal.

The band plays the final chorus of "All I Want for Christmas" and something, or rather someone, snags my attention across the room. His black hair is messy, and he is wearing dark jeans and a black T-shirt. He's the most casual guy in the room, but he's still earning glances from all the women around him.

I blink rapidly to clear my vision and make sure I'm not dreaming, but he's still there. *Beau* is here. He smiles when our eyes lock. I lift a hand in a small wave, half-convinced I'm just seeing things.

"Another dance?" Lucas steps back as the song changes to something more upbeat.

He starts to turn to follow my line of vision, but I grab his hand and pull him with me. "Actually, I need a drink. Let's join the guys at the bar."

Lucas doesn't need any more encouraging than that. He leads us off the dance floor and I dig my phone out of my purse.

With trembling hands, I read my missed texts.

> **Beau: I was at a party. Now I'm doing something spontaneous and a little crazy.**

A little while later, he sent another.

Beau: You look even more beautiful in person.

My fingers move over the keys at a frantic pace.

Me: OMG. You're here?!

My head spins.

"Not you two, too," Felix grumbles to Lucas as the two of us get closer.

"What do you say, Stell. Is that love I smell in the air for us?"

I don't respond right away because I barely heard him. *Beau is here.* I glance up at my brother and his teammates. This is so not good.

"We're just friends," I say.

"Ooooooh, burn." James holds a fist over his mouth as he laughs.

I shoot Lucas an apologetic smile. "But you're obviously the best choice here."

The guys cackle some more and my phone buzzes.

Beau: Yeah. Are you pissed? I should have warned you. It was a spontaneous decision. I couldn't wait to see you. I'm outside.

"What do you want to drink?" Felix asks.

"Just grab me a water when the bartender comes by. I'm going to run to the restroom and then I think I saw a friend from school."

"If she's hot and single, bring her over," Garrison says.

I force a smile. Yeah, I don't think that'll be happening.

I do stop in the restroom to check my makeup and take a few deep breaths. I send Beau a text that I'm headed to him and then I weave my way through the party, checking to make sure no one sees me go out the front door.

My stomach is in knots as I step into the cold night. Scanning the parking lot, I spot Beau leaning against a black SUV. He lifts a hand when our eyes meet. My stomach flips.

Among all the other emotions I felt at seeing him, excitement finally wins out now that we're alone. I jog toward him as fast as my stilettos will let me, without twisting an ankle.

He straightens and moves quickly, those long legs eating the space between us.

"Hi." I'm breathless when we're finally standing a foot away from each other.

"Hey." The Christmas lights strung around the resort reflect off his glasses. He still looks hesitant, like maybe he isn't so sure this was a good idea. Ditto, but he's here anyway.

I lunge for him, wrapping both arms around his neck. His arms go around my waist and he lifts me off the ground.

"Fucking finally." He exhales and then sets me back down.

We keep clinging to each other. He has several inches on me, so the position has me tilting my head up to look at him. His gaze drops to my mouth.

"I want to kiss you, but I can't decide if that's jumping about ten steps ahead since we haven't even held hands yet."

"I don't really like holding hands anyway," I say as my heart hammers in my chest.

One side of his mouth lifts as he leans in so close, I can smell the hint of peppermint from his gum. "Good to know."

Chapter Eleven

Beau

I DROP MY MOUTH TO HERS AND WE BOTH LINGER IN THAT position, neither of us pulling away or pushing for more. Frantic energy courses through me like a before-game rush. After a month of talking to this girl every day, she probably knows me better than anyone else, but this is only the second time we've ever been face to face.

Soft laughter slips from her lips, the movement and the sound vibrating against me.

A girl laughing while you kiss her isn't usually a good sign.

"Something funny?" I ask, resting my forehead against hers.

"No. Sometimes I laugh when I get nervous." She giggles again. "I can't believe you're here and we just kissed."

"Should I not have come?" I pull back to stare into her brown eyes.

"No. I'm glad that you did. All night I've been wishing you were here and now here you are." She waves a hand in front of me.

"You kinda like me, huh?" My lips curve into a smile and my pulse races.

Stella lifts up on her toes and slides her fingers through the hair at the back of my neck. "Just a little bit."

"Mmm." I brush my lips against hers again. "Let's see if we can change that into something more . . . enthusiastic."

Reaching down, I scoop her up. She squeals as her feet leave the ground. I love the feel of her silky dress and the sound of her sweet laughter as I slant my mouth over hers. The noises coming from her are sexy as hell. Her body grips tighter to mine as our tongues tangle.

Her heart beats rapidly and I'm breathless when she stops suddenly. "Half the Valley U football team is inside."

"I saw." I set her down but keep her close. "Should I be worried about Moore?"

"Lucas?" She laughs. "No, but we should probably stay out here."

Stella wraps her arms around her waist. I take off my coat and drape it around her shoulders.

"We can go anywhere you want," I say.

With a smile, she tips her head toward the front of the building. "If we sit close, we can hear the music."

Stella leads me to a bench off to the side of the front entrance. Some holiday tune plays, but I can't quite put my finger on the song.

When I take the seat beside her, she angles her body toward mine. "Why are you here? Really."

I rub my hands together in front of me. "I went to a buddy from high school's house tonight. An old teammate. We got to talking and I don't know . . . it all seemed so dumb. I like you; you like me. I'm only home for ten more days and I want to hang out. Who knows how long it'll be until we're in the same state again."

"Yeah." She nods slowly, as if she's thinking. Then her lips part and she hits me with a smile that has my heart rate picking up speed. "Yeah. You're right. It all seems so silly. I've been up here dying to see you and here you are. Of course, we should hang out. Do you want to go somewhere else?"

"Nah. I know you were looking forward to this. Has it lived up to your expectations?"

"Oh yeah. Did you see the decorations inside? Trees in every corner, gaudy wreaths, and lights." Her eyes widen. "So many lights. It's amazing."

"You really like Christmas, huh?"

"Of course. It's the best time of the year." She bumps her shoulder against mine. "How have things been at home?"

"Eh." I stretch my legs out in front of me. "More football and pep talks than holiday cheer, but that's really more our style."

"They're proud of you. They wouldn't push if they weren't, but I get it. I'm sorry."

I know she's right, but it doesn't make it any easier to sit through dinners where my dad replays every mistake I've made this year.

"You wanna dance?"

"Out here?" She grins.

"Or inside, whatever you want."

She stands and shrugs out of my coat, then sets it on the bench. Her fingers grip mine and she tugs gently. I get to my feet, and we come together again. Her hands on my shoulders and mine around her waist. We sway to the music and I hum lightly under my breath.

Leaning forward, she rests her head on my chest. I run a hand along the back of her head, then twist my fingers around her braid. Now this . . . this is my kind of holiday cheer.

"Stella?"

"Yeah?" She tips her head back to meet my gaze.

The words get caught in my throat. "Nothing. Just wanted to look at you again."

"Is that a line from a movie?" A playful smile dances on her lips.

"Probably." I chuckle. "What can I say? You're so gorgeous you make me want to spout cheesy lines."

While she's giggling, I wrap my arms around her tighter and take her mouth again.

Voices and the sound of footsteps coming out the front door

interrupt us. Reluctantly, I pull back but keep my arms around her. She sneaks a peek inside, and I suddenly feel like an ass for showing up and taking her away from a party she's obviously been enjoying.

"Maybe we should just go inside," I say as a man and woman head out to the parking lot, looking positively giddy.

"I don't think that would be a very good idea."

"All right, then." I take her hand. "I should go and let you enjoy the party."

"No. Don't go. You drove all the way here."

"I know how much you were looking forward to this and spending time with your brother and sister. It's fine. You'll be back in Scottsdale tomorrow, and we'll see each other soon."

She hesitates, but ultimately nods. "All right. Yeah. That'll give me time to figure out how we're going to explain you to my brother."

I grab my coat and we start for my vehicle. "I'm glad I got to see you tonight. By the way, I was right. Red was definitely the right call."

Smiling, she steps closer and wraps her fingers around my bicep. Her head tilts to the side and brushes against my shoulder. Disappointment settles on my chest. This didn't go down how I planned, but it was totally worth the drive to see her.

We're almost to my vehicle, and I'm dreading saying goodbye, when a deep voice calls out behind us. "Stella?"

Trepidation trickles down my spine as she grips my arm a little tighter.

"Ah, shit," I mutter. I wouldn't have thought I'd be able to pick out Felix Walter's voice without seeing his face, but the concerned edge to his tone is undeniably Stella's brother.

"It's okay," she whispers softly, and gives my bicep a reassuring squeeze. We freeze and she looks over her shoulder slowly before turning to face him.

Blowing out a breath, I turn and stand beside her.

"What's going on?" Felix asks. His gaze darts between us and I can tell the second he recognizes me. His jaw flexes and his eyes widen.

Three of his teammates hover behind him. They're talking, a couple of girls standing with them, all of them oblivious to me. Moore is the first to put the situation together. He moves to stand beside his QB.

"Is everything okay?" Lucas asks.

"I don't know," Felix says and takes another step toward us. "Stella, what's going on? Why are you standing next to Beau Ricci?"

The way my name rolls off his tongue, even I don't like myself right now.

"You piece of shit." Garrison Hamilton gets a wild look in his eye seconds before he rushes me, which is impressive for a guy wearing a boot. I pull Stella behind me and move closer to the madman coming at me, holding out a hand to stop him, which, of course, doesn't. He swings. I dodge at the last second, but he still manages to clip me.

I taste blood. Stella gasps behind me. I have no idea what is about to go down, so I put more distance between me and Stella to keep her safe.

"Stop it!" she yells when it looks like Garrison is coming back for another shot. She moves to my side, and he rethinks his attack.

I scan the area, weighing my options if they all come at me. Two more people join the commotion. I recognize both of them, but only know one. Theo Bradford. Valley U's star running back and Holly, Stella's twin.

Stella told me they were identical, but it's still trippy to see another version of my girl. This is not how I expected to meet her.

"Stella." Felix's icy tone cuts through the tension. I'm actually impressed with his ability to keep his cool. His teammates look like they want to murder me. "What the hell is going on?"

"Beau is the guy I've been talking to. We met at the airport.

Neither of us knew the connection at first," she says it all at once, like it can explain away any wrongdoing on my part.

"I have been dying to run into you off the field, Ricci." Garrison stalks around us. I don't like how close he's getting to Stella, but I don't know how to get her out of this situation. "Let's do this. Me and you."

"I didn't come here for a fight," I say, loud enough for them all to hear me.

"Too bad."

Garrison lunges at me again. This time, I'm prepared. I side-step, drawing him away from Stella. Then grab his T-shirt and hold him away from me.

"Fight me, you piece of shit," he yells.

"No!" My girl hurtles herself forward.

I let go of Garrison to shield her. What a clusterfuck. Felix finally joins the action. I think he's going to take a shot at me too, but instead, he gets between me and Garrison and tells his team-mate, "Take a walk before someone else gets hurt."

Garrison's voice is outraged. "He broke my fucking foot. My football career might be over because of this prick."

"You almost hit Stella. Take a fucking walk," Felix says again. "I need to talk to my sister."

I'm shocked when he listens. Garrison mutters some choice words to Felix, but then stalks off.

I glance back at Stella. Tears track down her face. Her sister has moved to stand beside her.

"I don't understand. What's going on?" Holly asks. It hits me then. Stella hasn't told her who I am. Confirmed by the look of hopelessness she sends me. My gut churns.

"We're just trying to figure out the same thing. Stella, please help me understand. Did you invite him here? Are you dating this asshole? Beau fucking Ricci, really?" Felix cuts me a hard look.

"She didn't invite me. I drove up to surprise her. She had nothing to do with this."

"I was going to tell you," Stella says to her brother. "This isn't how I wanted you to find out, but yeah, we like each other." She looks up at me, lips trembling. It does something to me to have her declare her feelings for me, a guy she barely knows, to her brother, who I know she cares about a great deal and also hates me.

That's not true. Yes, Felix hates me, but it isn't accurate to say that Stella barely knows me. In fact, I think she probably knows me better than anyone, but the reality is, this is only the second time we've met in person.

I wrap an arm around her and whisper, "I'm sorry."

I'm so fucking sorry I showed up here. It was selfish and reckless.

"No. This isn't happening. Stella, you can't date this guy. You know what he did to Garrison. Beau's dirty hit cost Garrison the season." Felix's words make me bristle.

"That was an accident." Stella swipes at the tears on her cheeks. I wonder if she's known all along. I wanted to tell her, but part of me does feel responsible. "He didn't intentionally hurt him."

"I'd never take a guy out on purpose," I say, more to her than anyone else.

"Yeah-fucking-right." Garrison stomps back toward us and gets in my face. "You expect me to believe that shit, Ricci? You fucking coward."

"You don't even know me." We've attracted an audience. Two guys, wearing security guard polos, come out the door and survey the situation. My mouth stings and I bring two fingers up to my lip and come away with blood. "I don't want to fight you, but I'm not walking away from Stella unless she tells me to."

I look down at her. "Are you okay?"

"She's not your concern." Felix practically growls the words and takes a step toward me.

"Okay, that's enough." All eyes go to Theo when he speaks. "We need to take this somewhere else before they call the cops."

Felix looks away from me and nods. "Agreed. We're done here.

It's time for you to leave, Ricci. Keep your dirty games to the field and leave my sister out of it."

The guys head for an orange Corvette at the front of the lot.

"Come on, Stell," Felix calls.

She worries her lip as she looks from him to me.

He says her name again.

"No," she says, finally. "This is dumb. You can't tell me who to date. Beau is a great guy. If you'd just take a breath and get to know him, you—"

"It's okay," I tell her. A knot forms in my chest. I can see the desperation, hear it in her tone, and I love her for it, but it's wasted tonight. "Go with your brother. We'll talk tomorrow."

"I'm sorry. This wasn't supposed to go this way."

She's right. And it's all my fault for showing up here. Dangerously stupid. More tears fall and I wipe them away with the pad of my thumb. "It's okay. Go, baby."

Chapter Twelve

Stella

I PLEAD WITH MY BROTHER ON THE RIDE BACK TO THE CABIN. Not that it does any good. I can see that everything I say in Beau's defense is being dismissed as quickly as the words leave my mouth.

I'm so mad, hot tears blur my vision. "You didn't even give him a chance!"

"You're catching me a little off guard here, Stell. You and Beau Ricci?!" I hate the way Felix says his name, like he's some terrible guy. He isn't. I refuse to believe that.

"Yes! He isn't the guy you think he is. He's funny and witty, sweet."

"Sweet?" He cuts me off before I can say more. "He has a reputation for being a player."

"He likes to have a good time."

"The guy is a wrecking ball, Stell."

"I know, I know. You think he took Garrison out on purpose. I don't believe that for a second. You don't know him like I do."

We pull up to the cabin. James is on the front porch with Garrison. The latter stomping around, shirt untucked. He's always been a little unhinged, quicker than my brother's other friends to get rowdy and start a fight. It's another reason it's easy to take Beau's side. If it were Teddy or Lucas, maybe I'd be more conflicted.

"Ah, shit," Teddy says. "I got him."

Felix turns in his seat. He looks tired and I feel a twinge of guilt. I should have told him before it went down like this.

"Let's talk about it tomorrow," he says.

"There is nothing to talk about. I like him. I'm going to keep seeing him."

"How do you know he isn't just using you to piss me and the guys off?"

I never even considered that, and I hate that it takes me a second to really reflect on the possibility. No, Beau would never do that. I give my brother a searing glare. "That's a low blow even for you."

I rush past the guys on the porch, straight back to the room Holly and I are staying in and start to pack. I don't want to be here anymore.

"What are you doing?" Holly asks as she walks in.

"I want to go home," I say flatly.

"Stell." Her voice breaks as she takes a seat on the bed. "You caught everyone by surprise. Give Felix the night to calm down."

"No. I can't stay here and listen to them talk about what a shitty guy Beau is." I can already hear them out there talking shit and I don't want any part of it. "He is a good guy."

Holly's voice goes quiet. "I believe you."

"You do?" I sit beside my twin.

"Yeah. I wish you would have told me who he was."

"I wanted to. I almost did a hundred times. But I didn't want you to have to keep something from Felix. It was hard enough for me." The three of us have always been close. Another reason that it hurts so much that Felix won't even consider that I might be right about Beau.

"What are you going to do?" Holly asks.

"I have no idea. But tonight, I want to curl up with Whiskers and sleep in my old bed." Our parents' cat is an adorable, fluffy white furball that loves to curl up on my chest. It's the best kind of therapy.

"Are you sure? We can stay in here, watch a movie in bed or get really drunk."

I smile at my sister. "I'm sure. I want to go home and wake up tomorrow and forget this entire trip happened. Please?"

She hesitates.

"Oh crap. I'm sorry. You want to stay for Teddy."

"No. I mean, yes, but it's okay."

"Holl—"

"If you want to go home, then let's go home. Whatever you need." She squeezes my hand.

Neither Holly nor I say much on the way to Scottsdale. We pull into the driveway of our childhood home just after two in the morning.

"Thank you," I tell her. I know she gave up time with Teddy to come with me and it means more than she could know.

"Of course. Come on. Everything will seem better in the morning."

I hope she's right.

Once I'm in my old bedroom, I change into sleep shorts and a baggy T-shirt and climb under the covers.

I plug in my phone. It's dying from the number of times I've checked for texts from Beau in the past three hours. He still hasn't sent anything. I try to FaceTime him, but there's no answer.

Me: I'm so sorry.

The dots appear a minute later.

Beau: You have nothing to apologize for. I shouldn't

have shown up like that. I hope you and Felix worked things out.

Me: Holly and I left. I'm in Scottsdale at my parents' house.

His reply starts and stops.

Me: Did you make it back okay?

Beau: Yeah. I made it back.

Me: Plans tomorrow?

Beau: We're going to my uncle's house in the afternoon. Probably be late before I'm home.

Me: Okay, what about the next day?

Beau: That's Christmas.

Me: Yeah. We'll be all celebrated out by dinnertime. I could come see you.

Beau: Maybe. Might have to play it by ear.

Me: Please don't let the things Felix said get in your head. We can figure this out.

Beau: Get some rest, baby. Talk tomorrow.

Me: Night, Beau.

Chapter Thirteen

Beau

CHRISTMAS EVENING EVERYONE COMES TO MY PARENTS' house for dinner. Mom has a ham in the oven and she and all the aunts are milling around the kitchen, cooking and shooing out anyone that comes in to ask when it will be ready. We had a chill morning opening presents and then went to brunch at my mom's parents' house. Tonight, it's Dad's family that is crammed into our living room.

I'm sitting right in the center of my uncles and cousins. It's chaos, not that I've really noticed, though. I'm in another world completely.

I can't stop thinking about Stella and the fight at the resort with her brother and teammates. I never should have showed up like that. Never should have gotten involved period, but Stella and I feel as unavoidable as snow in the mountains. Maybe if I'd never responded to those first texts, if I hadn't gotten to know her. But now it kills me to even think about not seeing her. And about the problems I've caused for her.

She sent a text this morning, but I haven't caved and opened it until now.

Stella: Merry Christmas!

She's all smiles in the picture, holding up a cat with a red bow stuck on top of its white head. I stare at it for several seconds before closing out with a groan. The first time I fall for a girl, and it had to be her.

"Food is ready," Mom says, wiping her forehead with the back of her hand.

Everyone jumps to their feet like the past couple of days haven't been one big meal after another. I'm not even hungry, but I fall into the back of the line and fill a plate with a little of everything.

The kids are shooed outside. We have a couple of outdoor heaters going to keep the space warm, but I don't mind the nip of cold in the air. Still feels balmy after spending so much time in Colorado. I take a seat next to one of my younger cousins, Scottie.

"When do you have to go back?" he asks, mouth full of potatoes.

"One more week."

He nods. "Think you might have time to practice with me?" The tips of his ears are pink.

"Yeah, definitely. How's football going?"

"Okay. I'm starting quarterback this year."

"I hadn't heard, man. That's awesome."

"I'm not really that good. Not like you."

I chuckle softly. "I wasn't always this good."

He shoots me a disbelieving side glance.

"I'm serious," I say. "Ask anyone. I was about a foot shorter than everyone else, weighed ninety pounds soaking wet, and had two left feet. It's just time and practice."

He shoves a forkful of mashed potatoes in his mouth. "So, you'll help me?"

My phone buzzes in my pocket. I rest my plate on one knee as I shift to get it.

> *Stella: Busy? I have five minutes before my family makes me play another board game.*
>
> *Me: Call me.*

"Yeah, kid. How about this weekend? Saturday?"

He thinks for a minute, as if he's mentally scrolling through his personal calendar. "That'll work."

I tap the bill of his hat when I stand. "I'll swing by and pick you up around noon."

I finish off what's left of my food on the way to the kitchen. My mom and aunts are still standing around, triple-checking things, refusing to eat until everyone else has had seconds. I fend off their attempts to get me to eat more because "they don't want leftovers," drop my plate, and head for my room.

Stella calls as I'm jogging up the last step.

"Hey," I answer, smiling when her face appears on screen. "Merry Christmas."

"Merry Christmas!" She pans the camera down to show me her sweatshirt, which reads, 'Buzz, your girlfriend is Woof!'

"I'm wearing red. Does that count as festive?" I point to the Cardinals hat on my head.

"No." She laughs. "Is your family still over?"

"Yeah."

I can read the disappointment on her face.

"It'll be an early night. What's your family up to?"

"We were playing board games, but then Teddy showed up to surprise Holly."

"That's nice." Something aches in my chest.

"He brought her a tree." She waits for me to react. "Like a Christmas tree. A real one because she was sad that we only had a fake one this year."

"That's . . . damn, that's romantic as hell." It occurs to me I've never bought a girl a Christmas gift. Not a real present. The cheeseburger I sent Stella suddenly doesn't feel so romantic. I might suck at this whole being a boyfriend thing. What a shitty realization.

"Right?" Her laughter cuts off, but she continues to smile. "Can you meet up in an hour or two?"

I swallow, pulse thrumming in my ears. I'm dying to see her

again, to hang out, to kiss her. Of course, I am, but I have this sinking feeling that I'm making things worse for her instead of better. Also, I don't really feel like getting hit again. In the end, my desire to see her outweighs everything else. "Yeah. I'd love that."

We head to a restaurant and bar roughly halfway between our houses. I get there first and then she pulls up in a Jeep and parks next to me. We both get out and meet at the back of her vehicle.

She's still wearing her *Home Alone* sweatshirt, paired with jeans and tall boots that add a couple inches to her height.

"Hi." She hesitates and then steps forward and hugs me.

I squeeze her tightly and then lift her off the ground, gaining a laugh out of her and easing the tension.

When I set her down, Stella rubs at her arms. "It's cold out. Do you want to go in?"

"Not really," I say. "I was thinking we could take a drive."

"Okay. Yeah, that sounds fun."

She gets in my car, or my dad's, since mine is parked in a lot in Colorado, and I take off toward familiar roads. It's quiet out tonight, most people home with their families.

I fiddle with the radio, almost every station is playing holiday music, so I unlock my phone and hand it to her. "You want to pick some music?"

She takes the device, staring down at it for a beat before she answers, "Absolutely. A person's phone is filled with all sorts of interesting secrets and details."

I chuckle. "Oh yeah? What exactly does my phone tell you about me that you don't already know?"

"Well, Spotify tells me that you recently listened to Mad Beats and Sick Workout Mix, so I'm guessing you mostly use the app when you're working out." She cocks a brow in question.

"That's true."

She puts on the Mad Beats playlist and then laughs when the heavy beat vibrates the seats.

"Not really a Mad Beats kind of vibe right now," she says as she quickly changes it.

"Aaron is always putting together new playlists for our gym sessions."

"Oh my gosh, Beau. You have over a thousand unopened emails!" Her eyes widen as she swipes through the apps on my phone. She groans. "You are one of *those* people who doesn't clear their notifications."

"Is that bad?"

"I have to clear my notifications or it makes me crazy."

"I think that says more about you than me," I tease, resting one hand on top of the steering wheel and moving the other to the gear shift.

She sets my phone in the middle console and angles her body toward mine, then takes my hand closest to hers and laces our fingers together.

I bring our joined hands to my lips and kiss the tips of her fingers. "How was your Christmas?"

"Good," she says cheerily, then a little more somberly adds, "A little weird. Felix and I aren't really speaking."

"I'm sorry."

"Don't be. He's being unreasonable."

My fingers squeeze the steering wheel a little tighter.

"Why didn't you tell me that you were the one who injured Garrison?"

"I don't know. Actually, that's not true. I thought you'd take their side. I wouldn't even blame you for it."

I glance over in time to see her nod slowly. "I watched it. I saw the play."

"I didn't mean to hurt him. I'd never do something like that on purpose . . ." I trail off, not sure what else to say.

190

A quiet beat falls between us. Stella speaks first. "You know, the funny thing is I think you and Felix have a lot in common."

"Because we both play football?"

"Not just that. You're both super competitive and extremely loyal. And you both deal with a lot of pressure from your family and teams. I've read articles about you. Your coaches and teammates all mention your work ethic and dedication."

"That's PR fluff. I work hard because if I don't, I'm letting a lot of people down. I don't have any choice but to be dedicated. We practice and lift every day, twice a day in the pre-season. We get January off, but February we're back on the field. You know what it's like being a D1 athlete."

"You say it like it's a burden."

"You don't feel that way?" I ask.

"No. I love it. I wish someone expected more of me."

"What do you mean?"

"Not all collegiate sports get the same respect as football. You guys are gods on campus. NFL players are celebrities. Can you name one gold medal diver?"

"Uh . . . no, but I've got a hot prediction for you." I wave my hand through the air. "Stella Walters, gold in the next summer games."

She smiles through an eye roll. "See?"

"I'm sorry."

"It's fine. I get it, but don't misunderstand that pressure. It means people care. A lot of people would love to have that care and attention aimed at them."

I hadn't really thought about it like that. Does it make it easier to take the criticism from my dad? No. But I get what she's saying.

I pull into a residential neighborhood that's decked out in lights. Each house is lit up, a couple even have it synced to music.

"This is amazing. You should see our house. Dad and Felix go all out every year. It's full-on Clark Griswold."

"And this isn't?" I point a thumb toward the brightest house.

"It definitely is. I love it."

I stop at the end of the cul-de-sac and pop open the glove box. "I got you something."

"You did?" Her mouth curves into a smile.

I hand her the small, badly wrapped present. "It isn't a Christmas tree."

"That Teddy, he did good." She runs a finger over the paper. "Should I open it now?"

"Yeah. If you want."

"I want." She tears into it with so much eagerness I wish it were something a lot more romantic.

She pulls out the black Colorado football beanie, still smiling, and puts it on.

"Just something silly. I have an identical one back at school."

"I love it." She touches the soft material on her head. "Thank you."

"You're welcome." I clear my throat, feeling a little embarrassed. Now that I've given it to her, it seems dumb. It isn't like she's ever going to wear it. Her brother might burn the damn thing.

"I love it, really," she says. "And I got something for you too."

"All I want for Christmas is you."

She laughs and cuts me a *could you be more ridiculous* glance.

"I know, I know. Cheesy but accurate, baby."

Stella pulls an envelope out of her purse and hands it to me. On the front is my name written in red and green alternating letters. I turn it over and rip the seal, then pull out two tickets.

"I know it's a long shot that you'll have time off, but conference diving championships are in February. If you can make it work, it'd be so fun to see you there. I can probably get you a Valley U beanie like this one." She points to the hat on her head.

My lips curl at the corners and I lean forward, brushing my lips against hers. "If at all possible, I'll be there."

I lean back and tap the tickets on the wheel and then put them back in the envelope. "Does your family go to your meets?"

"Some of them, not all. They'll all be there for the championships, though."

I'm still holding the envelope, a mixture of emotions swirling in my gut, when I ask, "Does your brother know you invited me?"

"No."

"Baby . . ."

"It will be fine," she insists, shifting closer to me. Her fingers thread through my hair and she brings her lips to mine.

I kiss her back, deepening it and giving her everything I have and then some. I like her. I like her a whole lot.

I don't have the same certainty about the future and navigating things with Felix and her family, but we're not going to solve anything tonight, so we might as well enjoy our time together.

Chapter Fourteen

Stella

I'M RUSHING OUT OF MY BEDROOM, SHOVING MY PHONE IN my purse with one hand and using the other to pull the door closed behind me. I'm also smiling like a fool because Beau is picking me up.

When I look up, Felix is standing at the other end of the hall.

"Hey," I say, trying to appear casual and like I'm not about to head out with his nemesis. I have on a dress and more makeup than normal, so I doubt I'm fooling him.

"Hi." His mouth opens and closes like he wants to say more, but he clamps it shut and his jaw flexes.

We've barely spoken all break. It isn't that I'm mad at him exactly, though it definitely still rankles how everything went down the night Beau showed up at the resort. But Felix is my brother. I love him, even when I'm angry with him. I think it's more disappointment. We're at an impasse. I don't want to stop seeing Beau, but I want things to be good between me and Felix, too.

"I thought you were hanging with Teddy tonight?"

"I did," he says. "He and Holly wanted to drive around and see the Christmas lights. I decided to call it an early night."

"Oh." I nod. That's the same thing Beau and I did a few nights ago. Except we only made it into one neighborhood before we were more interested in talking and kissing than looking at lights. I guess I understand why Felix wasn't into that.

"Where are you headed?" he asks. His tone and the hard set of his jaw tell me he already knows.

"Just out for a little bit." I adjust the strap of my purse on my shoulder. "I'll see you in the morning."

With that, I start down the stairs.

"Stella," Felix calls.

I take two more steps before I stop and look over my shoulder.

"Be careful," he says. "Call me if you need anything."

"Yeah." I swallow around a lump in my throat. "I will."

I jog toward the curb, pulling on the beanie Beau gave me last night, as he comes to a stop in front of the house.

"Hi." I climb in quickly and lean over the console to kiss him.

"Hey," he murmurs against my lips. His gaze flickers to the house and then back to me. He grins at my hat. "You look nice. I can almost picture you sitting on the sidelines cheering me on."

"Thanks. So do you." He has on jeans and a white T-shirt with a black leather jacket. Plain and casual, but so damn handsome. His dark hair is styled neatly and he's wearing the gold glasses I like so much.

"Where are we going?" I ask as he drives away from the house.

"It's a surprise." He lifts both brows in a playful waggle. His right hand leaves the steering wheel and rests on my knee.

I don't pay a lot of attention as he drives and neither of us says much. He turns up the music, and I enjoy the feel of his fingers brushing over my bare thigh and the way he bobs his head to the beat, occasionally glancing over to hit me with a smile. We've spent so much of our relationship talking, it's nice to be together and just soak it up.

Beau pulls off onto a gravel road. It winds about a half mile until we come to a scenic pull-off spot. It's dark, so we can't really see anything, but it has a serene feel and there are dots of color in the horizon from all the holiday lights in the distant neighborhoods.

He backs into a small clearing, gets out and rounds the front of the car, then opens my door.

"Where are we going?" I ask. I borrowed a pair of Holly's shoes, which make my legs look amazing but aren't great for hiking.

"Not far," he says. He pulls me to the back of the SUV and lifts the back. My jaw drops when I see the blankets and pillows spread out in the space.

One hand is in his front jeans pocket and the other rubs at his jaw. "Too cheesy? I just saw this for a second time how you must be seeing it. I just thought we could hang out and talk. This isn't me bringing you to a secluded spot to have sex. We could go out to eat or to a movie if you'd rather."

Laughing, I press my lips to his. "I love this, and if you don't try to feel me up in this dress, then I will be very disappointed."

I get in and sit, legs stretched out in front of me, looking out the back of the vehicle into the dark night sky.

He grins and climbs in beside me.

"Does your dad know you turned his vehicle into a shagging wagon?"

"The blankets were already back here." He pauses as if his words are slowly sinking in. "Oh man."

I burst out laughing. "I'm sure it's for picnics and such."

"Yeah," he grumbles. "Let's go with that."

He reaches for a thermos and two mugs, handing me one, and then filling both with hot chocolate.

"Marshmallows?" he asks, holding up a bag of the mini ones.

"Absolutely."

He sprinkles some into each of our mugs, then pops a few extra into his mouth. We sit shoulder to shoulder, sipping our drinks and staring out into the dark horizon dotted with lights.

"This is nice." I lean into him and let my head rest on his shoulder.

"Yeah." He sets his mug down and then shifts, so he's sitting behind me. My back rests against his front and my head is tucked under his chin.

I'm not sure I've ever been more content in my life. Sitting here with Beau feels like enough in a way I can't describe.

When we finish the hot chocolate, he turns on music and we talk about school, our friends, and college. We talk about everything until the only topic left is the one we've been avoiding.

"I saw Felix on my way out of the house tonight." I drop my gaze, not quite able to look him in the eye. I really thought he'd come around by now and each day he doesn't, it gets harder.

He gives me a small, apologetic smile. "I hate that I'm making things tense between you and him. I know how close you are."

"I don't know what to do," I admit. "I thought all he needed was time to get used to us being together. What if he never does?" The thought makes me nauseous.

"Maybe I should talk to him?" Beau offers.

"And say what?"

His chuckle is quiet and rough. "Yeah, good point. I don't know. I've been thinking, though, about what you said last night and about Felix, Garrison, that game, all of it."

I turn to face him.

"My playing football is everything to my family. It's three generations of hopes and dreams all looking to me to do the thing they couldn't or didn't get a chance to do. I know I'm not responsible for living up to that, but some part of me wants to, you know? It drives me, and maybe on occasion, it's made me sloppy and reckless, but I wasn't trying to take out Garrison."

"I know." I cup his cheek. "You're a good guy."

"Thanks," he says softly.

"I haven't met your family, but I doubt they know how their actions are impacting you."

His jaw works back and forth. He's told me his family isn't

big on talking, and I can see that now in the way he seems set to bury this and continue to let it eat at him.

"Are you planning on playing in the NFL?"

"I don't know," he says.

"I'm sure your family will want that, so you should probably just plan on it. Oh, and maybe you could be a broadcaster when you retire or even coach."

His brows tug together.

"My point is if you keep making decisions based on other people's happiness, you're going to end up with a life you don't want. And that's dumb. I hear we only get one of these."

A little of the tension eases in his features. "Okay, wiseass."

"I am very wise," I chirp. "You have to talk to them. Soon."

He nods his agreement. "What are you going to do after college?"

"I haven't planned that far ahead. Right now, I have my eye on a gold medal."

"Yeah?" One side of his mouth quirks up. "I knew it."

I get butterflies in my stomach just thinking about the possibility.

"My girlfriend is a total badass."

He takes my mouth and slides a hand behind my neck, his tongue seeking entrance immediately, and I climb into his lap. He drops his hands to my thighs and slides them up below the skirt of my dress.

My heart races and my core throbs. I arch into him and the ends of his fingers brush against my panties.

He groans as he drags a thumb over my clit through the damp material. I'm breathless as he breaks the kiss and stares into my eyes. Those green eyes see right into my soul.

I push his jacket off his shoulders and then go for the hem of his T-shirt. His upper body is broad and sculpted. I run my hands over every inch of his warm, toned skin.

"Do you have condoms?" I ask, still catching my breath.

His gaze searches mine. "Are you sure?"

"Yeah."

He closes the back of the SUV, and then as he gets a foil packet from his wallet, I pop the button on his jeans. Together, we push his jeans and boxer briefs down his legs.

My pulse races as I wrap my fingers around him. He's long and smooth and pulses under my touch.

Beau sucks in a breath. "Come here."

He grips me by the waist and brings me back onto his lap. We can't seem to fuse our mouths together tightly enough. My body tingles everywhere as we kiss, and I grind over him. My panties still keep us from being skin to skin, but it doesn't keep my orgasm from climbing to the brink.

When I'm delirious with it, quivering and shaking, he reaches for the packet and rips it open. I scramble to remove my panties as he rolls the condom over his length.

My chest heaves as we stare at each other in the back of the dark SUV. While he watches, I drag down the side zipper of the dress and then lift my hands to let him lift it over my head. He does and then I get another delicious groan from him when he realizes I'm now completely naked.

"You're stunning, baby."

I light up at his words and can't resist kissing him again. I rest my hands on his shoulders and he guides me down slowly until he's buried inside me.

"Oh, damn," he grits out. "You feel so good."

I let out a shaky laugh that sends a new wave of sensation through my core and Beau groans. His mouth fuses over mine and we get lost in more hungry kisses. I'm not sure which of us moves first, but soon, I'm rising and falling in a steady rhythm with his hands at my waist. We only stop kissing when the sensation gets too much, and I drop my forehead to his and let out a gasp.

"I'm so close," I tell him.

With that knowledge, his touch is rougher and his hips lift

to thrust into me from below. My orgasm is on a hair-trigger, detonated when he whispers my name in a guttural, throaty tone.

I cling to him, near sobbing with pleasure, and he follows me over the edge.

We clean up and then hang out a little longer, talking and kissing some more. But eventually, both of us are yawning and fighting sleep, so reluctantly, we move to the front of the vehicle, and he drives me home.

Beau parks in front of the house. It's dark, except for the Christmas tree that's still lit up in the front window. Everyone must have gone to bed.

"What are you doing tomorrow?" Beau asks.

"Nothing. Why?"

"You're going to Valley for New Year's Eve, and I leave the day after."

"Tomorrow is our last day together," I say. I knew our time was limited, but it sinks in with a heavy feeling in the pit of my stomach.

"For this trip." He brushes my hair away from my face and then runs his thumb along my trembling bottom lip. "Don't be sad. This has been my favorite Christmas vacation."

"Yeah. Same."

"I promised my cousin I'd toss the football around with him, but we should be done around lunchtime. Hang after?"

"I am going to see a play with Holly and my mom tomorrow night. We do it every year. I am free before that and maybe after."

"I'll take whatever I can get." He leans forward and slants his mouth over mine. "See you tomorrow."

The next afternoon, I pull into the parking lot of a middle school and drive back to the football field where Beau said he'd be. I can't see much of the field from the car, and he isn't answering his phone, so I get out and walk.

They're easy to spot once I get close, at least Beau is. He's surrounded by kids half his age and height. He's wearing shorts and a T-shirt that stretches over his broad chest and muscular arms. The way he runs down the field, easily catching a bad throw and then zig-zagging through the players makes a smile spread across my face.

I sit on the first row of bleacher seats and watch him. He looks so happy, so in his element that if I didn't know about the pressure from his family, I'd never believe it was possible his love for the game wasn't one hundred percent genuine.

After he carries the ball into the end zone, he tosses it to a kid who's probably around twelve with shaggy brown hair that Beau ruffles as he gets close. The kid sees me first, says something to Beau, and a second later, those green eyes find me. He lifts a hand in a wave and then runs over to me, sweaty and smiling big.

"Hey." He bends down to swipe his lips over mine. "Are you early or am I late?"

"The latter, but it's fine. I don't mind." I don't mind one bit.

"Give me five?" he asks.

"Of course."

"I want to let Scottie run it one more time, then I'm all yours." He winks as he jogs backward onto the field.

Chapter Fifteen

Beau

"THAT WAS INCREDIBLE." SCOTTIE'S LIPS SPLIT INTO a huge grin as he wipes his forehead with the bottom of his shirt.

His friends have already left, matching smiles on their faces. Mine too. It was pretty incredible. I can't remember the last time I had so much fun on the football field.

Don't get me wrong, winning with my team is satisfying in a way I can't describe. But this, just goofing around, having a good time, it's been too long since I've done it.

I walk with Scottie to the sideline where we left our stuff. He pulls on a hoodie while I drain what's left of my water.

"Is she your girlfriend?" His gaze is across the field where Stella still sits.

"Yep," I say, proudly.

"She's so hot. What's she doing with you?"

Laughing, I hit the brim of his hat. "I have no idea."

Together, we walk to her. She stands and smiles when we get close.

"Hey. All done?" she asks.

"Yep. Just had to show Scottie here how it's done." I tap a fist on his bicep. "Scottie, this is Stella."

"Hi," he says, his voice suddenly going quieter than it's been all morning.

"It's nice to meet you, Scottie." Stella smiles at him. "Nice arm. You have a real poised presence out there too."

His brows rise, like he can't believe a girl as hot as her knows anything about the sport. Ah, he has so much to learn.

"Stella's brother plays QB at Valley U."

"Your brother is Felix Walters?!"

"Yeah." She nods, laughing lightly. "You've seen him play?"

"Are you kidding? He's one of the best college quarterbacks in the country." He shoots a quick glance in my direction. "Dad said you guys have been playing against each other since you were my age."

"He's right."

"Oh, man. Maybe next time, he can come too. My friends would shit themselves."

I laugh. "Now there's an image."

Scottie takes off happily toward the car.

"He seems sweet," Stella says.

"He's a pretty cool kid. Thanks for not telling him that me and Felix aren't best buds. Might break his heart."

Stella leaves her Jeep, and we pile into my vehicle to drop off Scottie at his house, where I promise to practice with him once more before I head back to Colorado, and then we go back to my parents' house. They're both gone for the day. Dad's golfing and Mom went shopping with some of my aunts.

"Relax. They aren't here," I say as I open the door for her.

"Oh, thank god." She lets out a breath. "I mean, I'm dying to meet them, but I need more warning."

"Noted."

I show Stella my old bedroom. She smiles as she looks around the small space, then comes back and hugs me around the waist. Peering up at me, she asks, "Do they know about me?"

My lips twitch with amusement. "Maaaybe."

"Oh my gosh. Really?"

"Not all the details, but they know I'm talking to someone. You haven't told your parents about me?" As soon as the words leave my mouth, I nod. Of course, she hasn't. After the way Felix reacted, makes sense.

"Not yet." She lifts up on her toes to kiss me. "But I will, and they're gonna love you."

I lift both brows. I think she's overestimating my ability to win people over.

"Eventually," she adds.

"I love your optimism." I scoop her up and toss her on my bed.

We make out until her lips are puffy and her hair is disheveled. Damn, she looks good all mussed. I lift her T-shirt and place a kiss on her stomach. She sucks in a breath and looks down at me with a playful, naughty glint in her eyes.

I wiggle down her body, dropping more open-mouth kisses on the sensitive skin below her belly button. Slowly, I pop the button and then drag the zipper of her jeans down. She helps me get her pants off and then I settle between her smooth legs.

"I like these." I run a finger along the red, silky material of her panties, then hook a finger under the band and pull them down an inch.

She squirms under me. "You should take them off."

"Don't rush me, baby." I push her legs farther apart and hook an arm around one to hold her in place. Lightly, I rub her through the satin at a pace that has her casting a frustrated yet sexy stare at me.

I nip at her inner thigh and then glide my nose along her slit, breathing her in. Her panties show off how wet she is for me and it's the hottest thing. She's gorgeous and perfect and all fucking mine. I can't get over it. This stunning girl is mine.

I get it now. I understand why people do the relationship thing, want to spend all their time with one person, and are perfectly happy to shut out the rest of the world. Nothing feels better than being with Stella.

She's panting when I finally shove the damp material to the side and run my tongue from her ass to her clit, lapping her up along the way.

"Oh my gosh!" She threads her fingers through my hair and then gives the strands a tug.

It doesn't take much of me licking and sucking before her hips lift to create more friction. I hold her tighter and increase my efforts until she's saying my name and nearly ripping my hair from the scalp.

I pull every last bit of her orgasm from her and then her body goes limp, and she starts to giggle.

"That was . . . oh wow."

I wipe my mouth with the back of my hand and move up to lie beside her. She curls up on her side and nuzzles next to me. "I'm never leaving this bed."

"All right." I crook a hand behind my head. "Makes my plans to kidnap you and keep you with me easier."

She giggles again and then sits up quickly and straddles me, still wearing only her T-shirt and her sexy red panties with a giant wet spot.

I stare at her, wondering how I got so damn lucky. "I have a surprise for you."

"Oh, yeah." Her brows lift and she moves so that she's rubbing against my dick. Oh, damn that feels good.

As much as I don't want to, I lift her off me and grab my laptop. She sits cross-legged on my bed while I pull up the movie. The look on her face when she sees what I've chosen is priceless.

"*Home Alone 2*. That's my favorite."

"I know. I remembered."

"Holly likes the first one better, but there's just something about this one."

"I still haven't watched it." I hit play, and we sit side by side, leaning our backs against the headboard.

"It's so good," she promises and drapes a leg over mine.

I spend as much time watching her reactions to the movie as I do watching it myself. I don't get to observe her like this, in the little moments just living life and going about her days, and it tugs at something in my chest.

We get about halfway through before her phone starts buzzing. The first two times I don't say anything when she silences it, but I hit pause when it goes off the third time.

"I'm sorry," she says. "It's Holly."

"You have to go?"

She nods. "Maybe I can duck out early."

"Nah. Don't be silly. It's your yearly tradition."

"What are you going to do tonight?"

"Not sure. I'll probably call a buddy from high school. Better than sitting around here waiting for my dad to get on my case about not going to the gym enough over break."

"You haven't talked to him yet?"

I shake my head. By the time I got up this morning, both mom and dad were already gone for the day. Not that I probably would have brought it up anyway. It's hard because, on the surface, things are fine. If my dad notices that I grind my teeth every time he offers up advice on upping my game, he hasn't mentioned it. And it's just easier not to start a fight when I'm only home for a couple more days.

"He means well," I say to defend him. I don't want Stella to think either of my parents are bad people—they aren't.

"I'm sure he does, but their actions are affecting you in a real way. You need to talk to them."

"We don't do that." I give her a half-hearted grin and then concede. "I know."

"They can't read your mind. You love football, don't let them make you hate it."

206

"I love it, huh?"

"I saw how happy you were out there today with Scottie. Cute, too. I can't wait to watch you in a real game."

"That was different." As soon as I say the words, I wonder if that's true. And if it is, why.

Her phone buzzes again.

"Come on. You're going to be late."

She sighs and sits up, then pulls her jeans back on. Before she stands, I duck my head under her T-shirt and give each boob one more kiss. I'm gonna miss those. I'm gonna miss the woman attached to them.

"Okay, but this isn't goodbye. I'm going to see you again before you go back. We'll figure it out." She scrambles off the bed, adjusting her clothes and smoothing a hand over her hair. She hits me with a sad smile and holds out her hand to me. "Don't you dare leave Arizona without seeing me first, Beau Ricci."

"I promise," I say, getting to my feet and following her down the stairs and outside. We don't speak as I drive her back to her vehicle. When I pull up beside it, she lunges for me over the console, kissing me like that isn't what we did all afternoon. Not that I'm complaining, but she's seriously going to be late, and her family already doesn't like me.

I hold back a groan as she opens her door to get out. "I could stay here for New Year's Eve."

"I thought you were celebrating Felix's birthday that night too."

"We are, but we're barely speaking to each other." She lifts one shoulder and lets it fall.

"You have to go. You know you do. He's your brother."

"And you're my sexy boyfriend who is leaving in two days."

"Baby, no."

"Do you not want to spend New Year's Eve with me?"

"Of course, I do."

"Then what's the big deal? Felix's actual birthday isn't until the third. Plus, I'll see him all semester, but who knows when I'll see you again."

"He already hates me. I don't want to give him another reason."

"So, you're going to miss spending time with me to try to make up for everything else? That doesn't make any sense."

"It's his birthday, Stell."

She's frustrated. Hell, I am too, but I know I can't let her skip that party. I slide a hand around the back of her neck and press my lips to hers once more. "I promise I will see you again before I leave town, okay?"

She nods her head ever so slightly.

"You better go. I'll call you later."

Without a word, she gets out and into her Jeep. I watch her drive off and then finally let out a long breath, letting the forced smile fall from my face. Fuck. This sucks.

Chapter Sixteen

Stella

"A RE YOU OKAY?" HOLLY ASKS AS WE WAIT IN LINE FOR the bathroom during intermission.

I check my phone to see if I have any texts from Beau. I don't, and shove my phone back into my clutch with a little more force than necessary. "Yeah."

"Liar. What's going on?"

"Tomorrow we go back to Valley and then the next day Beau leaves for Colorado. Christmas vacation is over."

"You made it work before this, you two will be fine."

"Yeah, but that was before . . . everything."

She gives me a sympathetic smile.

"I think I love him, Holly."

"Oh, Stell." She wraps one arm around my shoulder and squeezes. "That's good news. I'm so happy for you."

"Then why do I feel so awful?" The back of my eyes sting with tears I refuse to shed in public.

"Did something happen today? You seemed fine earlier."

"I told him I wanted to stay here for New Year's Eve and he said no, that I should be there for Felix's birthday."

"First off, I would be so sad if you missed it. So would Felix. We always ring in the new year together. And second, he's right. He doesn't want you to do something you'll regret."

"It's not even his actual birthday."

"That's semantics and you know it."

"Why doesn't he want to spend his last night in Arizona with me?"

"I'm sure that he does."

I'm not so sure. I've brought as much drama to his vacation as I have fun. Maybe he's decided I'm not worth it and this is his way of letting me down easy. He's made no bones about the fact he isn't a relationship guy. And now he's in one and we can't even go to a party together because my brother hates him.

My head spins and I can't make heads or tails of the thoughts racing through my brain. Irrational or not, I worry that the happy, fun bubble Beau and I have been living in has officially popped.

As soon as we get home from the theater, I text him.

> **Me:** *Home. Want to come over?*
>
> **Beau:** *To your house?*
>
> **Me:** *Felix isn't home. He's gone for the night.*
>
> **Beau:** *How about we go to a party? I'll pick you up in twenty minutes.*

He takes me to the house of a friend, of a friend from high school. The place is huge and the backyard is filled with people. Beau introduces me to his friend Lonnie and a bunch of other people he went to school with.

He isn't drinking, but fills a cup of foamy beer for me. I sip it as we mingle. Even sober and not playing any games, he is the life of the party. Guys pat his back and bump his fist, eager to hear how he's doing and offer congrats on his season, while girls bat their lashes and send him not-so-secret smiles.

"Do they not see me standing here?" I ask, after one hugs him a little too long and tells him to call her sometime.

"They're just being nice."

"Mhmm."

"Damn you're sexy when you're jealous," he whispers in my ear and then kisses down the column of my neck. He pulls back to stare into my eyes. The look he gives me takes the wind out of me, but before he says a word, a familiar form snags my attention across the yard.

"What is he doing here?" I mutter.

Beau follows my gaze to where Felix and Teddy stand next to the keg.

"They went to a bowl game. He's not supposed to be in town," I say, mostly to myself. My sexy boyfriend takes a step away from me, and the look on his face is something close to shame or maybe guilt.

It breaks my heart for him. And for me, if I'm honest. I want to bring him home and introduce him to Holly and my parents, go to parties without worrying about who we'll run into. I want to stop sneaking around. Beau deserves that. He's done nothing wrong.

"I'm gonna talk to him," I say. "I'll be right back."

"No." Beau grips my hand tighter. "I'll talk to him."

Chapter Seventeen

Beau

Stella's fingers clasp around mine. Felix and I are having a stare down. I'm trying to figure out what the right thing to do is, and he looks like he wants to pummel me and then hand me off to Teddy to finish the job.

She looks like she wants to argue with me, but I give her my most reassuring smile. "It needs to be me."

I give her one more squeeze and then cross the yard toward her brother. He sees me coming, but holds his ground. His lips are pressed into a hard, straight line, and he turns to have a conversation with a group of guys nearby.

He didn't automatically come running over to bash my face in, or really act in any visible way like he cares I exist, and that should be enough, but it gnaws at me.

I second-guess myself with every step closer. The party is huge. We could probably avoid each other with a little luck, but this is my girlfriend's brother. If I don't make peace with him, how is it ever going to work? I know deep in my gut that it won't.

At five feet away, I cross my fingers that this doesn't turn out like the last time.

Teddy nudges him as I get close, and Felix turns toward me. I watch as his face morphs from happy and relaxed to pissed right the hell off.

"Hey," I say. "Can we talk?"

"I don't have anything to say to you, Ricci." His gaze briefly skims to place his sister, and he lifts his hand to wave to her, a ghost of a smile replacing the glare he was just giving me. He starts to turn back around but Teddy juts his chin in my direction and they do some sort of silent communicating.

Taking two steps away from the group, he says, "You have thirty seconds."

I follow, intentionally leaving space between us. "I like Stella. A lot."

His jaw flexes.

"I'm not playing her or using her to piss you off. I genuinely care about her. Can't we squash this shit between us?"

"This shit?" He takes one small step closer. "You hurt one of my teammates. You're reckless and careless, and that's just on the field. I've known you a long time, a lot longer than Stella has. Your reputation off the field isn't exactly stellar either, Ricci."

"I'm not denying any of that. I've made mistakes. I'm not perfect, but you don't know me. Not really."

Maybe he's right. No, he's definitely right. I don't deserve Stella, but I want her all the same.

"I know enough." He sidesteps to leave.

"I'm in love with her," I say, heart pounding with words I haven't said to anyone before. I don't know when it happened; maybe I was in love with her all along, and it just took spending time with her in person to realize it, but I'm absolutely certain.

He faces me, brows lifted in surprise.

"I am in love with your sister, man," I repeat, in case he needs to hear it again. "So, hit me or whatever you want. I need to make things right between us for her."

His jaw works side to side, like he's mulling over my words, but he doesn't say anything before he turns and leaves me there, still uncertain where we stand.

"I'm sorry about tonight," Stella says as we sit in my dad's car outside of her house.

"Nah, don't be. I'm glad we got to hang."

After I talked to Felix, we tried to make the most of the night and stay at the party, but neither of us was really feeling it.

She shifts closer and rests an arm around my neck, her fingers playing with my hair. "I had a really good vacation with you."

"Yeah, same." My throat feels tight as I swallow. Felix's orange corvette is in the driveway. I should be concentrating on saying goodbye to my girl, but my mind is conflicted.

Felix is never going to approve of me. I get that now. I don't know what I'm going to do about it, but I get it. Eventually, she'll get tired of defending me or resent not being able to have us all together without drama. In the end, I know she'll choose Felix. And if she doesn't, she'll regret it.

"Are you okay?" she asks.

"Just tired."

"Me too. I better go." She leans forward and kisses me, then hits me with a smile before she gets out of the vehicle. "Call me in the morning. Maybe Holly and I can swing by on our way back to Valley."

"Okay." I fake a convincing enough smile that she shuts the door and waves as I pull away.

As I drive off, I can't help but think that maybe this is where things should end. I can't be that guy that forces her to choose between me and her family. She deserves more than that.

Chapter Eighteen

Stella

THE NEXT DAY, I DRIVE BACK TO VALLEY ALONE. HOLLY decided to ride with Teddy, and they left early this morning. I predict this semester I'm going to see a lot less of my twin in our shared dorm room.

I waited until after ten, hoping I'd be able to see Beau one last time before I left, but when he finally texted me back this morning, it was to say he was practicing with Scottie and wasn't sure what time he'd be done.

Saying goodbye sucks. I think I'm going to drive back tomorrow and see him off at the airport. It's a lot of driving for a short amount of time, but I already miss him.

When I get back to Valley, I head straight to my brother's to help set up for the party later tonight.

I knock and then walk through the front door. Holly and Teddy are on one end of the couch, Lucas the other.

"Hey, Stella," Lucas calls when he sees me.

"Hi." I give a small wave to everyone. Felix is standing in the kitchen, drinking a protein shake. He nods his welcome. We're still not in agreement about Beau, but we stayed up late last night playing video games and talking until the weirdness between us faded.

I really, really like Beau. I'm not willing to give him up, but I don't want to keep fighting with my brother, either.

"I thought the place would already be decked out for tonight," I say, taking a seat in the empty armchair.

"We're picking up the keg later," Lucas says.

"Wait, this is it?" Holly asks, voice rising in disbelief. "What about decorations?"

The guys share a confused look.

"Oh my gosh, you need decorations!" She throws her hands up in the air.

The guys laugh, but fifteen minutes later, the five of us are hanging up streamers and blowing up balloons.

It takes very little to get Lucas excited about the prospect of decorating. He and Holly take the lead, Teddy follows Holly, of course. I don't know how she ever didn't see how crazy he is about her. I find myself alone with Felix as he picks up the kitchen and goes through their liquor stash to figure out what they still need to buy.

"Are you expecting a lot of people tonight?" I ask as I sit on a stool in front of the counter.

He nods as he places a dusty handle of Wild Turkey in front of me. "A decent number of guys on the team are back, so I expect we'll have a good turnout."

"I got you something." I slide off the stool and go to my purse to retrieve the gifts I got him. I hand him the leather key chain with his name and football number on it first. "Sorry, I didn't have time to wrap it."

"Thank you. This is awesome."

"I also got you this."

One corner of his mouth lifts as I set down the beaded shot glass necklace. He puts it around his neck and turns on the flashing neon light. "Thank you, Stell."

He takes it off and sets it on the counter next to the liquor.

"Beau helped me pick both of them out."

He avoids my gaze as he asks, "Did you see him before you left?"

"No. He was helping his younger cousin practice some football drills this morning. I'm going to drive up tomorrow and see him off at the airport."

He nods slowly and then braces both hands on the granite between us. "I'm sorry about how everything went down this break. I know you were hoping we were going to be BFFs."

"I didn't hope that."

One of my brother's dark brows lifts.

"Okay, I kind of did. I thought if you got to know him, you'd see what a decent guy he really is, but you wouldn't even give him a chance."

"I heard him out."

"Not really."

"Sure, I did. He told me that he cared about you and that he wanted to squash all the bullshit for you."

I squirm with the squishy way those words make me feel as well as the scrutiny in Felix's gaze. "I care about him too."

"It's hard to explain, but I'm just leery of the guy, okay? I can't help it. I can't magically erase every bad thing I've ever heard or thought just because you say he's all right."

"No, I understand."

"You do?"

"I think your view of him is incredibly surface-level, but sure, I can see how Beau comes off as a guy you wouldn't want me to date." And yeah, knowing Beau better, I can see why Felix had the initial reaction he did, but those things aren't all that Beau is.

I can tell I've caught my brother by surprise, so I keep going.

"He feels a lot of pressure from his family to succeed, and I think that's why he comes off as reckless on the field. They look at him as the chance none of them ever had and he doesn't want to let them down. It wears on him. But, Felix, that's such a small part of who he is. Just like you being a great quarterback is a fraction of who you are.

"Beau is funny and sweet. He's the kind of guy who plays

217

football with his young cousin and his friends, just to make their day, and the kind of guy who sends cheeseburgers instead of flowers because he gets me." I realize I'm basically pleading with him to see Beau in a different light (which is highly unlikely), but I can't stop. "And I get him too, which is why I'm asking you to just consider that maybe there's more to him than you think. And if that doesn't work, then know this, I am crazy about him. More than crazy. I love him. It isn't some crush that is going to fade in a few weeks.

"But I hate that things are weird between us. You're my favorite big brother."

His mouth twists as he nods. He wraps one arm around my neck, and I hug his middle. "Me too. I'm sorry. I will try to wrap my brain around him not being a terrible human."

The others come in from outside and the moment is broken, but hopefully, he'll think about what I said. For now, though, it's time to get this party set up.

After we finish decorating the guys' house for tonight, they head out to pick up the keg and more liquor, and Holly and I go back to our dorm room to get ready.

"What's Beau doing tonight?" Holly asks as she curls my hair.

"He's going to dinner with his family and then to a party at some guy's house from high school."

She meets my stare in the mirror and gives me a sad smile. "I'm sorry. It has to suck not being able to spend his last night in Arizona together."

"Tonight will be fun." I put on my brightest smile. "I can't imagine not being here for Felix's birthday. Beau and I are going to FaceTime when it gets close to midnight, and then I'm going to crash, so I can drive back early tomorrow morning and see him before he flies back to Colorado."

"That's sweet. I want to meet him sometime."

"You do?"

"Yeah, of course. I've told you that before."

"Right, but that was before."

"I still want to meet him. I didn't push over break because I knew you were enjoying alone time you never get."

"Plus, you were busy making out with Teddy."

A blush creeps up her neck. "And that."

"Did you two make it official? Is Theodore your boyfriend?"

She nods and a proud smile stretches across her face. "Yep. I can't believe it."

"Well, I can. You're great and he's always been crazy about you."

"It's still so weird." She shakes her head. "I'm so happy."

"Me too," I say. And I am. Mostly.

Three hours later, I'm sitting in the dining room at Felix's house. I'm more of an observer of the party than a participant, but since everyone is in that happy tipsy state, I'm practically invisible.

> *Me: Maybe I should just come up tonight? I doubt anyone will miss me.*

> *Beau: You know that isn't true. What's Holly doing?*

I glance around the room. Holly and Teddy are on the make-shift dance floor in the living room. Teddy has one big, possessive paw on her hip, and Holly has been smiling for so long, I think her face is permanently stuck like that now.

I don't know where Felix went. Probably outside. There's a group out there playing washers.

> *Me: Dancing with Teddy.*

> *Beau: Go dance! You love to dance. But tell Moore to back off my girl.*

I laugh and then a pang of sadness hits me in the gut. I already miss him so much.

Me: I miss you. <pouty face>

He replies with a selfie of him making an actual frowny face and then another text.

Beau: Go have fun, baby. I'll call you at 11:59.

For the next two hours, I do just that. My twin is smiling so big as she and Teddy shout the lyrics to a Taylor Swift song to each other. Adorable.

But another pang of sadness hits me that Beau isn't here. I try to brush it off. So, we won't be together, at least I'll get to ring in the new year with him. The reality is, if we're going to be together, it's going to be like this—talking on the phone, texting, FaceTiming through important events. I wonder how much a plane ticket is to Colorado?

I sashay off the dance floor and pull my phone from the bust of my dress. I'm checking the driving distance to get to Beau, in case I want to take a spontaneous road trip to visit him at college next semester, when I spot Felix near the front door. He's surprisingly sober for it being his birthday, but he is holding a fifth of Jack in one hand, so I'd say he's aiming to take care of that.

He beckons me with a tip of his head.

"Hey," I say, letting out a long breath and looking around. More people than I expected showed up tonight and his small house is packed. "Some party. It's almost a new year. Any resolutions?"

"Yeah." He runs a hand through his hair, leaving the dark strands sticking up. "A few. You?"

Before I can answer, someone yells, "Five minutes!"

My phone buzzes in my hand at the same time Felix says, "Can you get the door?"

"The door?" I glance down at the screen of my phone, not surprised at all that it's Beau calling.

"I think the doorbell just rang."

"I didn't even know you had a doorbell," I yell, but the noise level has escalated as everyone prepares to ring in the new year. I walk toward it and as I'm opening it, I say, "Wait. Why am I opening your door? You live here."

He shrugs, and with an eye roll, I look to the other side of the open door.

My breath catches and then my stomach does several somersaults. My boyfriend stands on the other side. His face lights up, which makes my stomach do another flip.

"Beau?"

His smile dims slightly as he looks past me to where Felix stands. I glance between them and my excitement quickly dissolves. *Oh no.* I can see the drama about to unfold, just like at the resort. Why is Beau here, and how do I get us out of here before shit goes down?

Beau doesn't make a move to come inside, and Felix holds his ground. I take a step toward my boyfriend.

I'm not sure what I expect him to do, but he wraps an arm around my waist casually like him showing up is no big deal, and says, "Hey, baby."

Chapter Nineteen

Beau

STELLA STANDS STIFFLY NEXT TO ME, HER GAZE BOUNCING between me and her brother. Everyone else at the party is too busy to notice me, which I'm thankful for in this situation.

Stella sends a pleading glance to her brother. Something that looks like, *please don't kick my boyfriend's ass tonight.* From her lips to God's ears.

"Happy birthday," I say to him.

He gives a quick chin lift. "Thanks. You two should stay outside or you can hang in my room. Garrison isn't here, but other guys on the team are, and the more they drink, the less certain I am they won't try to start something."

"I appreciate it." I was shocked to get a text from him earlier tonight, inviting me to come down tonight for Stella. Even more shocked that it wasn't a trap. Although, I guess this could be phase one of a very elaborate plan.

Felix nods. My girl's gaze keeps darting between her brother and me as she tries to piece together what's happening.

"You did this?" she asks Felix. "You invited him?"

He doesn't answer, but she rushes him anyway and hugs him around the neck. "Thank you."

"Three minutes!"

Felix takes a step back, gives me one last not-quite-murderous-but-not-exactly-friendly stare, and then joins the others counting down to the new year.

Stella practically bounds over to me. "I can't believe you're here."

"Come on." I take her hand and we go out the front door. It's a nice, clear night, and the stars twinkle down on us.

"I'm stunned and so happy." She beams up at me.

"Me too."

We walk around the house, through a gate, and into the backyard. Holly and her boyfriend are standing on the far side, a few others by a keg in a red tub, but Stella and I stay off by ourselves. I'm wearing a plain white baseball hat pulled down low over my eyes, not exactly incognito, but showing up in CU gear seemed like a bad plan.

"You look amazing." I slide my hands around her waist and clasp them behind her back.

"Holly did my hair and makeup."

I remove one hand from her back to twist a finger around a red curl. She tips her head to lean into my touch.

"What'd your family and friends say about you leaving the night before you head back to college?"

"I changed my flight to stay a couple more days."

Her eyes widen. "Really?"

"Yeah." I chuckle and squeeze her to me. "You know, I want to get in another practice with Scottie, and my dad and uncles are going to watch the Cardinals game tomorrow."

She squeals and bounces in my arms.

"What do you say? Want to go to a football game and meet my crazy family?"

"Yes! Definitely."

"Good. We have three more days and I want to spend every minute of them with you."

"Yes! Yes! Yes!" She kisses me with all that enthusiasm, and I give it right back. When I made my holiday travel plans months ago, I never dreamed I'd want to extend my time at home. Now I'm dreading going back.

I move one arm down to scoop her up and bring her closer. She giggles, but keeps kissing me. My chest tightens. How does one person change your life so much in such a short amount of time?

Shouts from inside indicate we're in the final seconds of the countdown. I set Stella down and pull the sparklers out of my back pocket. "I brought these."

With swollen, wet lips, she takes them from me with a stunned expression on her face.

"Are you okay?" I dig the lighter out of my front pocket to light the sparklers.

I step closer, flick the lighter on, and bring it to the end of one, colorful sparks lighting up the dark between us.

"I love you."

My gaze lifts and a slow smile raises the corner of my lips as her words sink in.

"I love you too."

A chorus of cheers come from inside.

"Happy New Year!" she says.

"Happy New Year, baby."

I take her mouth and we bring in the new year the same way I hope to end it. I don't know how I'll manage not seeing her and kissing her for weeks or months at a time, but that's a problem to figure out later. Tonight, tomorrow, I'm just going to enjoy this.

When we break apart, Holly is standing a few feet away, smiling at us.

"Happy New Year," she says to her sister and then they embrace, Stella holding the sparkler away from her body.

I give Teddy a nod, and he surprises me by reciprocating.

"Sparklers?" I ask and offer them a couple.

"Yes, please." Holly gives me a big smile.

"You saved me, man," Teddy says. "Thanks."

"Yeah, of course."

Inside, they're singing "Auld Lang Syne" and Holly and Stella sing along, waving their sparklers around and making sparks fly, both of them smiling.

Someone in the neighborhood shoots off fireworks and our heads lift to watch the colors explode in the sky.

Stella comes back to me and wraps her arms around my middle. She tips her head up to look at me. "Best night ever."

"Definitely," I agree.

"Ready to get out of here." A new kind of excitement lights up her features, and she presses her boobs into me. "My dorm is in walking distance."

"Walking?" I scoop her up. "How long will it take us if I run?" She laughs.

"Good to see you both," I say to Teddy and Holly.

Holly lets out a quiet laugh. "Good to see you, Beau."

"Bye. Love you," Stella calls to her sister.

"Let's get breakfast tomorrow," Holly calls, as I start for the gate with my girl.

"I'd like that," I say at the same time Stella says, "We'll see."

For the next seventy-two hours, Stella doesn't leave my side. I introduce her to my family, we hang with Scottie and his friends, we go to the Cardinals game with my dad and uncles, and every second I get her alone, well, that's between me and her.

The morning I have to leave, she drives me to the airport and walks with me to the security gate. We linger next to the line, holding on to one another.

"I don't want you to go."

"Me neither." I tip her chin up and look into her watery, brown eyes. "Five weeks and I'll see you at the diving championships."

"And six weeks after that is spring break," she adds.

"Exactly. And in the meantime, I'll be blowing up your phone."

"You better." She nuzzles into my chest.

I hold her until I'm in danger of missing my flight.

"All right. I gotta go. I love you."

"I love you too." She wipes at a tear and then steps back.

I wipe it away with the pad of my thumb, and then brush a quick kiss on her lips.

I turn and walk toward the security line. I glance at her one last time and wave before I hand the guy behind the podium my ID and ticket. My heart feels full and heavy at the same time.

My flight is boarding, but it isn't my turn yet, so I take a seat and pull out my phone. I just stare at the screen. A second later, it lights up with a FaceTime call from Stella. I hit accept quickly.

"Baby?" I answer, thinking something is wrong. Or maybe I forgot something.

"I love you," she says as her face fills the screen. "I just needed to say it one more time. Have a safe flight."

I sink back in my chair. "I love you too. Wanna keep me company until they force me to put away my phone?"

She grins. "Absolutely."

Epilogue

Beau

One year later—Christmas

I RING THE DOORBELL AND STEP BACK TO TAKE IN THE SHEER number of Christmas lights and holiday displays on the Walters family house.

Stella warned me that they went super over the top this year, but her description did not do it justice.

I'm still taking it all in when the front door opens.

"Hey." Felix tips his head in greeting. "You made it."

He opens the door to let me in and I hold back a chuckle. If the outside of the house is over the top, the inside looks like something straight out of a Christmas catalog.

My gaze roams, noting the decorated trees in every room, more lights strung up inside, as well as wreaths and holiday pictures—it even smells like Christmas in here.

"Oh, come on," Felix says, snagging my attention. He waves a hand in front of my T-shirt. "You can't wear that."

"What, this?" I ask, fighting a grin as I stare down at my football championship shirt.

We met Valley in the conference championship game earlier this month and pulled out a victory. It was close. Felix threw the kind of game that will be talked about for years to come, but we were better. At least that day.

"Is that Beau?" Stella calls from the kitchen.

Felix is still grumbling under his breath, so I holler back, "Hey, baby."

A second later, she comes running and jumps into my arms.

"You're finally here!" She peppers me in kisses, and I give them right back.

I don't hold back in front of Felix. We've reached a sort of understanding. I do right by his sister, and he doesn't try to murder me. Seems fair.

I place Stella on the ground when her parents join us. Mr. and Mrs. Walters are cool. I think they might even like me.

"Hey, Beau," Mrs. Walters says, "Merry Christmas."

"Merry Christmas." I hand over the tin of cookies my mom forced me to bring. "These are from my family."

"That's so nice." Stella's dad pops open the top and takes one out. He bites into it with a satisfied smile. "Are you any good at board games?"

"Uh . . ."

"He's on my team." Stella tugs me into the dining room. There's a stack of board games on the floor. Holly and Teddy sit on the far side.

"Hey, Beau," Holly says. Now, the twin sister I have won over. Maybe even her boyfriend.

"Hey, guys. Merry Christmas." I extend a hand to Teddy and take a seat across from him. "What are you playing?"

"We just finished Scattergories," Stella says. "Holly destroyed us."

"Nice." I offer her a fist bump, and she grins proudly.

We play Scrabble next, followed by Cranium. Mr. and Mrs. Walters call it a night after that, and the five of us head into the living room to watch a movie.

Holly sets a tray of cookies on the coffee table. "*Jingle All the Way* or *Home Alone*?"

"*Die Hard*," Felix says.

"We watched that one two nights ago," Stella says. "Let Beau pick."

"Uhh . . . I haven't seen either of them."

"What?" All four of them look at me with wide eyes.

"The TV at my house is either on football or Hallmark." I shrug.

Felix grabs a cookie and waves it around as he speaks. "Let's do *Jingle All the Way* tonight. We don't have time to watch both *Home Alone* movies. We'll do that tomorrow."

"He's seen the second one," Stella says, and then blushes. "Or part of it."

"You guys don't have to do that. Watch whatever you want."

Felix kicks back and rests his bare feet on the table. "It's too late, Ricci. You wanted to date a Walters, well, that requires cramming as much holiday cheer as possible into every day between Christmas and New Year's."

I smile as I look around the room and a lump forms in my throat. It's a peace offering. Not the first, but one that feels a hell of a lot more significant than the others.

"All right, yeah. Let's do it."

Stella snuggles up next to me and we watch the movie all the way through. When it's over, everyone disappears, leaving us alone in front of the TV.

"How was Christmas with your family?" she asks, covering a yawn.

I play with a strand of her hair, curling it around one finger. "It was good."

"And things with your dad?"

"That's good too. He's barely said a word about football since I've been home. It's almost freaky."

"You miss talking about it with him, don't you?"

"Kind of." I chuckle.

Last summer, about two years later than I should have, I finally talked to my parents about the pressure I was feeling with football and how it was impacting my love of the game. My dad barely spoke to me for a week. I was sure we'd never see our way through it, but slowly, we're finding a path forward. One where we communicate a little better. It hasn't been one big conversation; it's been a bunch of small ones. We're both more comfortable tossing a football around than talking about our feelings, but I'm glad I said something.

I never would have without Stella. I owe her a lot.

"I got you a present." I get up and get my coat to retrieve the small box from my pocket. She wore the hell out of the beanie I got her last year. She even wore it to my game against Valley (though she had on a Valley U T-shirt too). But this year, I stepped up my gift game.

She tears open the paper carefully and then lifts the lid off the black box.

"Beau!" she gasps. "These are beautiful."

She lifts one of the diamond star earrings and holds it up to her right ear. My girl isn't big on jewelry, but these are simple and stunning, just like her. She puts one in each ear and then tucks her hair behind them. "How do they look?"

"Gorgeous." I press my lips to hers.

"I got you something too," she says, pulling back just enough to get out the words.

"You can give it to me later." I slant my mouth over hers and deepen the kiss. The only thing I want for Christmas is her.

Cheesy as hell but absolutely, one hundred percent accurate.

Acknowledgments

These books were such a fun project for me. I have wanted to write holiday books for a few years now, and they brought me even more joy than I expected.

I have so many people to thank. First off, to my favorite twins, Shari & Jess. You two are in all my favorite childhood memories. Thank you for that and for being the first people to encourage me to continue writing.

Thank you to Kristie at Between the Wines Consulting for helping me plot these stories. It was such a joy to talk to you, and your insight was gold!

My dream team—Anelise, Becca, Becky, Katie, Nancy, and Sarah—my books are better because of you. Thank you for all you do!

Special thanks to Amy, Catherine, and Kristy for being the best co-workers a girl could ask for.

Thank you to Devyn for all you do, Nina and everyone at Valentine PR, to Lori Jackson for these fun, gorgeous covers, and to Stacey at Champagne Formatting for the interior.

Finally, thank you so much to every reader and influencer who picked up this book. Your support means so much to me.

Also by
REBECCA JENSHAK

Campus Wallflowers Series
Tutoring the Player
Hating the Player
Scoring the Player
Tempting the Player

Wildcat Hockey Series
Wildcat
Wild about You

Campus Nights Series
Secret Puck
Bad Crush
Broken Hearts
Wild Love

Smart Jocks Series
The Assist
The Fadeaway
The Tip-Off
The Fake
The Pass

Standalone Novels
Sweet Spot
Electric Blue Love

About the Author

Rebecca Jenshak is a *USA Today* bestselling author of new adult and sports romance. She lives in Arizona with her family. When she isn't writing, you can find her attending local sporting events, hanging out with family and friends, or with her nose buried in a book.

Sign up for her newsletter for book sales and release news.

www.rebeccajenshak.com

Made in the USA
Coppell, TX
03 May 2023

16364366R00136